Adventure USA

ALASKA!
Danger on the Mushing Trail

Book 1

BARBARA LARMON FAILING

Illustrations by Erik Drohman

FORESTDALE PRESS, LLC

Copyright © 2023 by Barbara Larmon Failing
Forestdale Press, LLC

All rights reserved.

Book cover design, interior design, and illustrations by Erik Drohman
Developmental editing by Pam Glauber
Additional editing and proofreading by Sirah Jarocki and Taylor Morris

This is a work of fiction. Names, characters, places, organizations, and incidents are either the product of the author's imagination or are used fictitiously. Any resemblance to actual persons, living or dead, business establishments, events or locales is entirely coincidental.

No part of this book may be reproduced in any form or by any electronic or mechanical means, including storage and retrieval systems, without written permission from the author, except for the use of brief quotations in a book review.

eBook ISBN: 978-0-9916509-0-3
Paperback ISBN: 978-0-9916509-3-4
Hardcover ISBN: 978-0-9916509-2-7

Forestdale Press, LLC
715 Shawan Falls Drive
Suite 654
Dublin, OH 43017

For Robert

ALASKA!
Danger on the Mushing Trail

ALASKA

TABLE OF CONTENTS

1. Hawk River, Alaska 1
2. Man's Best Enemy 6
3. Honey Balls and Fatty Meat 12
4. *Hike!* 21
5. A Mean Shadow 30
6. Hank 36
7. The Sprint 46
8. Popsicle 57
9. Dr. Josh 62
10. Trailblazing 68
11. Snapping to the Gangline 72
12. Apprentice Musher 76
13. Injured 83
14. Marooned 87
15. A Dangerous Plan 91
16. Trouble on the Trail 95
17. Disaster 99
18. It's Up to Josh 102
19. Snowmobile 109
20. Across the Field 114
21. Winner's Circle 118

Please review 129
Glossary 130
Thinking about ALASKA! Danger on the Mushing Trail 132
Acknowledgments 135
About the Author 137
Adventure USA Supports One Dublin 139
Sneak preview:
   Book 2 - MASSACHUSETTS! The Stolen Spyglass 141

CHAPTER 1
Hawk River, Alaska

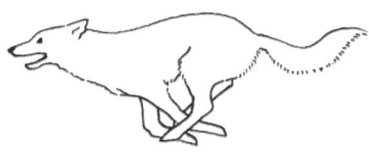

"It's a blizzard!" eleven-year-old Josh Parker cried. He stood by the window searching for the thermometer outside his cousin's house in Hawk River, Alaska. The barren landscape of snow-covered fields stretched as far as he could see. In the distance, sled dogs howled. Immediately, his heart began a rapid beat. Without thinking, he rubbed a faded pink scar on his wrist.

In the swirling snow, Josh could barely read the thermometer. He pushed his curly blond hair off his face and put his Phillies cap on backward.

"My guess is twenty-five degrees!" called his twin sister, Lizzie. "That's twenty-five degrees *above* zero, Oshy."

ADVENTURE USA

"Wrong, Lizard. It's twenty," said Josh. "I win the bet." He snatched the last donut hole from the kitchen table and popped it in his mouth.

Lizzie slumped in her chair and twirled her long, wavy brown hair. "Hey! I thought for sure that last one was mine."

"Nope," said Josh with a grin.

"I guess the weather here is nothing like the weather you're used to in New Jersey," Uncle Bob said to Josh as he handed his wife a cup of coffee.

Aunt Terry took a sip. "And when was the last time your family saw snow there at the beach?"

"Never like this!" said Josh.

Josh and Lizzie's parents, Mike and Sue Parker, wrote a popular eco-travel blog, which frequently had the family out exploring. The previous day, they had flown into Anchorage, Alaska, for two weeks tacked onto a school vacation. Josh and Lizzie were staying with their favorite aunt and uncle while their parents researched the Kenai Peninsula.

"Can we make some more donuts?" asked Lizzie.

"Sure," said Aunt Terry. "But what about school?"

"Not much to do, just extra credit," said Lizzie. "I already downloaded the assignments."

"I'm glad we're not Zooming," said Josh. "It took forever for the browser to load."

"The internet is often spotty," said Aunt Terry.

"And cell phone service is the same."

Their sixteen-year-old cousin, Brent, galloped down the steps. "Time to check on the dogs. Come on, Josh. Let's go meet the team."

"Okay," Josh said, careful to hide the tremor that crept into his voice. He didn't dare glance at Lizzie. He knew what she was thinking.

"You want to come too, Lizzie?" Brent asked.

"Not right now," she said, glancing at Josh. "I'm staying here where it's warm."

Fine, Josh thought, trying to ignore the lump in his throat. *I can do this alone.*

In the mudroom, Brent reached for a pair of boots that had thick rubber soles for traction. He slipped in mukluk liners to make them warmer.

Josh looked down at his hiking shoes and frowned. "I guess these aren't the best."

"They're fine for walking around town, but for mushing, you want a warm sturdy boot," Brent said. "Frostbite is a real threat. We have extras of everything. Mittens, parkas, hats. You choose."

Josh grabbed his parka and a pair of thick mittens from the shelf. He pulled out the Phillies ski hat his mom had gotten him for the trip and switched it with his ball cap. *For luck*, he thought. "Where are the dogs anyway?" he asked.

"They're outside, of course! In the dog yard." Brent put on his parka. "Alaskan huskies like it cold. With two layers of fur, they're made for it." He pulled a wool gaiter over his head to keep his neck warm. "I'm a sprint musher. The races are shorter—30 miles or so. I've been training the team for the county finals. In a few years, I might think about the Junior Iditarod."

Brent zipped up his parka. "Ready?" He opened the door, letting in a blast of frigid air. "Let's go!"

Josh wrestled with his zipper, his heart doing push-ups as he followed Brent out the door.

Fresh powder coated the trees near the house, their branches stretching into the cloudless blue sky. Immediately, the dogs started howling.

Josh felt like he was living a nightmare. His mouth was so dry that he could barely swallow.

Up ahead in a large fenced yard, the dogs yipped with excitement on their tethers. The closest one, a black-and-brown husky, bared her teeth. She looked exactly like a small German Shepherd. She jumped left and right as though she had springs on her feet.

"Hey, Vortex," said Brent, entering the dog yard. "This is Josh."

Josh's heart still pounded a rapid *dum-dum, dum-dum* as he inched toward the fence. *Please*, he silently begged, *don't let me blow this*.

But as Brent unclipped Vortex, the dog shot out of the yard. She flew toward Josh, hitting his chest with full force, knocking him down.

"No! No!" Josh cried. "Not again!" He thrust his fists up to protect his face, unable to control his panicked screams.

Brent was there in a second, grasping Vortex's collar and holding her back. "Easy, Vortex. Maybe too much enthusiasm for a first meeting. Right, Josh?"

Josh jerked away and tore off toward the house, furiously wiping away his tears.

"Hey, Cuz," Brent called. "C'mon. Vortex just wants to make friends."

When Josh reached the side door, Lizzie was waiting inside. He turned back to Brent and saw what he'd been dreading since they'd arrived. Brent looked concerned, but there was something else.

Disgust.

Brent sees me for what I really am, thought Josh.
A loser.

Chapter 2
Man's Best Enemy

Lizzie's eyes were full of compassion. "I'm so sorry, Oshy."

Josh shook his head and went into the bathroom, where he splattered cold water on his face. It did little to hide the red blotches. *Why did Mom and Dad think this trip to Alaska was such a great idea?* Taking a deep breath, he walked down the hall.

Uncle Bob sat at the dining room table, a plate of fresh caramel donuts in front of him. "I saw Vortex gave you her extra-exuberant hello."

Josh nodded, not trusting himself to speak and appear even more foolish.

"How about a warm donut?" asked Aunt Terry.

Josh breathed in the delicious aroma, but he was too upset to eat. "I'm good, thanks."

"This can't be your first incident with a dog," said Brent, taking off his parka.

"It was a German Shepherd." His heart pounding, Josh pushed up the sleeve of his shirt to expose the scar on his wrist.

"Was she sick?" asked Brent. "Super protective?"

Josh was silent, unable to say more.

"We were playing Frisbee with Roxy, our neighbor's dog," called Lizzie from the living room. "Suddenly, she went *chomp*!"

Josh remembered the searing pain and then the blood. He gazed out the window. "I needed stitches," he croaked.

"I get it." Brent put his hand on Josh's back. "But I'd trust my life to my dogs. I'm sure they wouldn't hurt you." He paused. "Man's best friend."

Josh took another deep breath. If only his cousin were a skier, a snowboarder, or a snowmobile racer. Any sport but one that involved man's best *enemy*.

Aunt Terry came out of the kitchen. "Time for school," she said. "I promised not to nag, but it's better to work on those assignments a bit each day instead of leaving it all for the end."

Normally, Josh would have found an excuse, but at that moment he was grateful for the distraction. "We could pick a topic for that Alaska report."

ADVENTURE USA

"How about the Iditarod?" Brent asked.

"What's that?" asked Lizzie.

"A sled dog race that's over a thousand miles," Brent said.

Josh flopped in a chair. "Who'd want to go a thousand miles on a dog sled?"

"Mushers and their dogs," said Brent. "There was a diphtheria epidemic years ago, and they desperately needed antitoxin medicine. All the ports were frozen, so they used railroads and sled dogs to get the medicine from Nenana to Nome. They called it the Serum Run. Some people feel the Iditarod commemorates it."

Brent sat on the couch. "Joe Redington founded the Iditarod. He wanted to promote sled dogs and have the Iditarod Trail certified as a national historic trail."

Josh perked up. "Sounds interesting. I like history."

"Somewhere upstairs there's a copy of *Champion of Alaskan Huskies*," Brent said. "A ton of information in it."

"I call the Iditarod!" cried Lizzie. "And I can include photographs of some of the dogs."

"Guess I'll do mine on Joe Redington," said Josh.

Later, after the twins had put in time on their reports, they headed for the card table set up near the fireplace. Uncle Bob had laid out a jigsaw puzzle of Denali National Park. The twins worked on opposite sides of the table.

Brent came in from the barn. "How about a sled dog ride?" he asked.

"Yes!" cried Lizzie. "Just what we need after all that work."

Josh thought fast. A ride was the last thing he wanted. But the dogs would all be harnessed, right? And they'd be attached to the sled, so maybe it wouldn't be another disaster. "Sure," he said, forcing some enthusiasm.

After they suited up in their warm clothing, Brent lifted a box down from the shelf above the coat hooks. Inside were a variety of ski helmets. "Pick one that fits," he said, putting his on over a thin fleece cap. "It'll keep your head protected and extra warm. And we have goggles in the barn."

The twins tried on the smaller ones.

"Perfect," said Lizzie as Josh put his on too.

Brent opened the door. The frosty air felt like a sucker punch. Immediately, howling from the dog yard started up.

Reluctantly, Josh followed Brent and Lizzie through the snow. The silo with *Parkerview Farm* written on its side towered into the sky. A small red flag fluttered from the top.

Lizzie rummaged for her phone. "The flag waving and the silo will make a great opening scene for my first blog post. I'm so glad Mom helped me set it up." Lizzie filmed a quick video clip. "And we finally got phones."

"With a ton of restrictions," added Josh.

"But a good camera."

ADVENTURE USA

Josh took his out. "No service, though."

Suddenly, a rusted pickup truck roared up the driveway. The driver jerked the vehicle in front of the barn, parked, and hopped out, a black husky right behind him.

Josh couldn't help shrinking back.

"Hey, Hank," Brent called. "What's up?"

"Back inside, Sable!" Hank yelled at the husky. When she ignored him, he picked her up and thrust her into the truck. "These dogs never listen!" he cried.

Turning to Brent, Hank asked, "You guys have any dog food you can spare? Those huskies eat way too much. I was due for a delivery yesterday, but it never arrived."

"We've got plenty," said Brent. "I can help you load it."

"Thanks," said Hank as the two walked toward the barn.

Lizzie and Josh watched as they loaded several gigantic bags into the back of the truck.

"Thanks, buddy," said Hank.

"Any time," said Brent.

As Hank opened the door, Sable tried to jump out again, but he pushed her back into the cab.

Frowning, Josh watched Hank's truck race down the driveway. "I thought mushers liked dogs."

"Hank's just moved back from Otter Falls near Fairbanks," said Brent. "He's trying to build his mushing team here.

Can be stressful." He turned toward the dog yard. "C'mon! Let's organize the team."

There was only one thing Josh wanted to organize: a non-stop flight back to New Jersey.

Chapter 3
Honey Balls and Fatty Meat

The huskies slept in brightly colored, rectangular wooden houses with flat roofs. Each house had a swivel post beside it, and Brent had tethered each dog with a chain to the pole, allowing them to exercise.

"Some people wonder about tethering the dogs," said Brent. "But it helps them have their own space. They also run around off their chains and socialize in that large free-run area on the other side of the barn."

The dogs continued to howl and wag their tails. Sweat trickled down Josh's back despite the raw cold. The flurry of dogs was dizzying. Their raucous yips broke the air like explosions.

Honey Balls and Fatty Meat

A teenage girl in a silver-and-black hooded parka walked toward them carrying two five-gallon buckets.

"Hi there!" called Brent over the noisy dogs. "The team knows it's dinnertime."

Resting the buckets on the ground, the girl raised a mittened hand into the air. "Hey, guys!"

"This is Atasak, a fellow sprint racer," said Brent. "And super skilled too."

"Thanks. I'm pumped about my recent times."

"What's the latest?" asked Brent.

"I shaved off a couple of seconds in the last few practice runs."

"Nice," said Brent. "Sometimes the winning time comes down to those extra seconds." He turned toward the fence. "These are my cousins, Lizzie and Josh."

Josh inched closer as Lizzie waved hello.

"Atasak is a big help," said Brent.

"I try." Atasak looked down, her long black hair falling over her face. "Did you hear my dad fell on the ice?"

"No! What happened?"

"He was fishing and slipped at Blue Lake." Atasak pushed her hair back as she met Brent's eyes. "I need to pick up some more hours."

"We can help. How about a weekend shift? I can talk to my parents."

A grateful smile appeared on Atasak's face. "That'd be wonderful."

"Let the Association know too. I'm sure others could use your help."

"Why was your dad fishing now, when it's so cold?" Lizzie asked.

"I'm Inuit, one of the Alaskan native tribes. We live off the land by fishing and farming. It's called subsistence." Atasak gestured to her coat. "My mom made my parka from sealskin.

Honey Balls and Fatty Meat

And I made my mittens." She paused. "My brothers can help, but no one fishes like my dad. We may have to buy food. But we'll need money for that." She turned to Brent, changing the subject. "How's Thunder?"

"Much better," he said.

She breathed a sigh of relief. "You can't afford to have any issues right now."

"What happened?" Josh asked.

Brent shrugged. "Thunder threw up twice last week. I kept a close eye on him. Caught him eating snow. That told me it was most likely winter blap disease."

"Blap? That's a funny word," said Lizzie.

"It's a strange name for a serious problem," explained Brent. "After exercising, dogs will occasionally eat wheelbarrows full of snow. Minutes later, they'll throw up everything in their stomach." Brent leaned a shovel against the fence. "It can also happen in the summer after drinking too much water."

"Then it's summer blap?" Josh asked.

Brent nodded as he pointed across the dog yard at Thunder. "There he is. The big black-and-white one. He looks just fine now."

All the while, the dogs had been howling, but seeing the food buckets, they sprang up and down, pulling on their tethers. Lizzie took out her phone and started filming. "This is great action!" she cried.

ADVENTURE USA

After taking the video, she pocketed her phone and peered into one of Atasak's buckets. "What's for dinner?"

"Some people use dry food because it lasts longer," said Brent. "But I prefer raw food for my dog team. Chicken, lamb, beef, salmon, and vegetables if I can get them. Much healthier."

"Today we'll feed them frozen fish mixed with water," Atasak said, "because it's above zero. Fish are perfect because they're mostly water."

"That's to keep them hydrated, right?" said Josh.

"Exactly," said Brent. "How did you know that?"

"He reads *all the time*," said Lizzie. "I'm surprised you don't have a book with you right now."

Josh pulled a slim copy of *Running Dogs* out of his pocket and smiled sheepishly.

Lizzie rolled her eyes. "See what I mean?"

"The more I know, the better," muttered Josh.

"Well, you're right about the water," said Brent. "Winter is very dry. I have to make sure the dogs drink enough. But not too much. It's tricky."

Brent took one of Atasak's buckets, and the dogs grew even more excited. "The dogs stay on their chains while they eat. Then there's no fighting for food."

Each dog house had a large metal bowl set into a wooden frame and attached to the side of the house.

Honey Balls and Fatty Meat

"When it's freezing, we thaw the meat first," continued Brent. "After I feed them, I circle back to where I started and take whatever they didn't eat. We train them to eat quickly before the food freezes in the bowl."

Brent and Atasak moved from house to house, putting food in the bowls. Josh watched the dogs' teeth as they gobbled up the food, easily tearing and gnashing the fish. *No way am I getting anywhere near those daggers again*, he thought.

"When I'm racing, they get power snacks," Brent went on. "Honey balls made of powdered eggs, honey, vitamins, and fatty meat rolled into a ball the size of your fist. Sometimes I roll in frozen beaver too. They love it."

"Yum," said Lizzie. "Maybe you can have that for breakfast tomorrow, Josh."

"Yuck!" he said.

"How many dogs do you have?" Lizzie asked Atasak.

"Ten. But I'd like to get a few more." Atasak reached for the shovel. "My turn today." She turned back to the twins. "Poop duty."

"What?" Josh's jaw dropped open. "You have to clean up the dog yard?"

Atasak nodded. "It's the worst job. But if you love dogs, you don't mind as much. And it's so much easier in the winter since they freeze into poopsicles." She waved. "See you guys later."

The twins wished her luck on poopsicle duty as Brent put away the buckets. He turned to the twins with a nostalgic grin.

ADVENTURE USA

"I got my first sled when I was seven. Back then, we only had one dog. Eventually, I added many more dogs and got a bigger sled."

Brent motioned toward two black-and-white huskies. "Those are my lead dogs, Midnight and Thunder. They're fast runners and good at obeying commands."

"Midnight's eyes are a brighter blue," said Lizzie.

Josh had the same thought. Huskies had eyes like wolves. Much scarier than a dog.

"And Thunder's ears are shorter," added Lizzie.

"Who cares? They're *beasts*," muttered Josh.

"All dogs come from wolves," said Brent. "But huskies look more ferocious." He scanned the dog yard. "See those two white ones by the side fence?"

"The ones with a little black on their ears?" asked Lizzie.

Brent nodded. "The one that's mostly white is Popsicle. The other is Boots. They run in second position. They're my swing dogs. They help lead or swing the dogs around turns."

Brent pointed to the left side of the dog yard. "And those brown-and-black dogs over there?"

A shiver went through Josh. He knew exactly who Brent was pointing at.

"They look like German Shepherds," said Lizzie.

"That's right." Brent laughed. "They're my wheel dogs, Vortex and Nova. A little bigger and stronger than the rest."

"They act like wheels?" Lizzie asked.

Honey Balls and Fatty Meat

"Not exactly. But they do balance us. They get around obstacles by pulling wide around tight corners. It's their job to make sure we don't tip over. They feel the turn of the sled the most."

"What about the others?" wondered Lizzie.

"The rest are team dogs. They can run in whatever position they're needed. Usually ahead of the wheel dogs."

Lizzie bent down to let the dogs smell her. Then she took off a mitten, reached out, and rubbed her hand through their thick fur.

Brent pulled his hood over his helmet. "We've got time before the county finals meeting. Let's go mushing!"

"Yay!" Lizzie said.

"Josh?" Brent asked. "You up for it?"

"Um..." Josh started. He wanted to ask about the harnesses, wanted to be sure he wouldn't be attacked again. But he didn't dare. "Sure."

"Nice," said Brent. "And no worries about Vortex. She was overly excited. Shouldn't happen again."

Yeah, right, Josh thought as he caught up to Lizzie.

"Knock, knock," he said.

"Who's there?" asked Lizzie.

"Bark."

"Bark who?" she asked.

"Bark yourself next to me, and you'll be safe," said Josh.

ADVENTURE USA

"I *am* safe. You're safe too." Lizzie smiled. "You have to believe Brent."

Chapter 4
Hike!

The twins followed Brent into the barn. He pointed to a large hook where a bunch of goggles hung. "Get a pair and stretch it over your helmet, so it's ready for use."

After the twins positioned their goggles, they passed a set of rustic shelves that held a sleeping bag, several axes, headlamps, and a tall, partially rusted metal bucket.

Josh picked it up. "What's this?"

"My cooker," Brent said. "An old friend gave me his when he stopped mushing." Brent pulled out a metal loaf pan from a large rectangular opening at the bottom of the cooker. "You put methanol in here with a little straw if you have it. It gets burning hot when lit."

ADVENTURE USA

He removed the lid from the top of the cooker and pulled out an inner metal bucket. "Food or snow goes in here, which cooks or melts very quickly. The inner pot must be large enough to boil three gallons of water. You can even make spaghetti. On the trail, I mostly eat freeze-dried food. But I also use the cooker to thaw food for the dogs."

He turned back to the shelf. "All these items are essential to mushing and staying safe." He held up a roomy cloth bag. "Here's my dog bag in case a dog is sick or injured and needs to be transported. I've only needed it once, thank goodness."

Josh picked up a headlamp. "This looks like something you'd need in a cave."

"That might be the most important piece of equipment. It's hard to hold onto a flashlight in subzero wind chill." Brent turned it on and flicked a switch. "There's a wide flood light for hitching up dogs or organizing gear, and there's a focused spotlight to see where you're going on the trail. The lead dogs can be sixty-four feet or more in front of you."

Josh's eyes got wide.

"Wow, that's really far!" Lizzie exclaimed.

Brent put the headlamp back on the shelf and picked up a small package. "Extra batteries. You always need them in your emergency bag. I keep the headlamp charged, but once I almost ran out of light on the trail at night. I took a wrong turn—easy to do in the dark—and got home just in time. Hypothermia, the lowering of your body temperature, can be deadly."

Brent moved to the other side of the barn. "Let's get the bigger sled ready." He pointed to a heavy braided rope hanging on the wall. "Josh, lay that gangline straight out on the snow while I get the harnesses."

Lizzie headed for the sled. It was eight feet long and made of curved flexible wood with heavy plastic runners. Lined with rope netting, it resembled a collapsed basketball net. Lizzie easily pushed it toward the door but had trouble moving it around a large barrel as she turned. An arched piece of plastic at the front of the sled tapped the barrel.

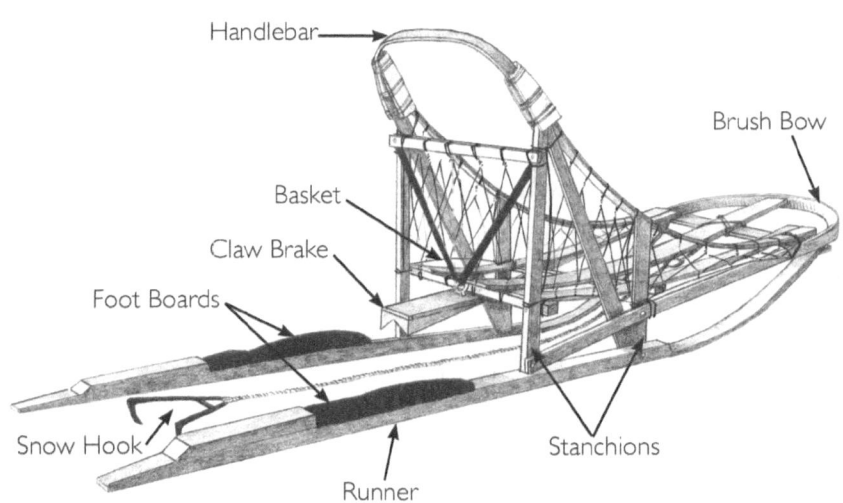

"Oops," she said.

"That's what the brush bow is for," Brent said. "Stops brush from damaging the sled. Sort of like a car bumper." He brought out the harnesses. As soon as the dogs caught sight of them, their plaintive howls rose to a frantic roar.

"I guess they're excited to go," said Lizzie.

"They're sled dogs." Brent worked quickly to lay out the lines. "They're made to run."

"How do you stop this thing?" Josh asked.

"Use the brakes." Brent showed him the flat metal piece attached to the back of the sled. "When I step on it, the claws on the bottom slow down the sled. There's also a drag brake between the runners."

Josh picked up a heavy piece of metal attached to the sled with a rope. It had two U-shaped prongs and sharp points like teeth. "This is the snow hook, right?"

Brent nodded. "If the snow is deep and firm, I can drive it into the packed snow, and it will hold the team for a little while. Go ahead and press it into the snow and then stomp on it."

Josh did as Brent directed.

"Nice work, Cuz," said Brent. He held up another rope. "This is the snub line. When the snow is soft, I can tie off and anchor the team to a tree."

Josh backed up as Brent began to harness the dogs. Their impatient barks were still deafening. Brent took hold of

Midnight's collar and unhooked her. He put the harness over her head and then lifted her strong front legs, neatly fitting the harness on her body. Next, he made sure it was flat and correctly positioned.

"I always check to be sure the weight of the pull is on the dog's shoulders and chest," Brent said.

He harnessed the rest of the dogs and then held up a cable attached to the gangline. "This is the tug line," he explained as he used the tug lines to hook the dogs in pairs on either side of the gangline.

Josh watched as Midnight hopped back and forth over the gangline with excitement. Suddenly, there was a growl from the middle of the line.

Immediately, Josh was thrown into the memory of that terrifying afternoon. They had been playing Frisbee with their neighbor's German Shepherd. One minute they were tossing the Frisbee back and forth, Roxy soaring into the air to catch it with her teeth. Then Lizzie tossed it closer to Josh. He stretched to catch it, colliding with Roxy. This was her Frisbee, and as she lunged, her strong jaws snapped to capture it. But Josh's wrist got in the way. It was only his quick reflexes that saved him from a more disastrous injury.

"Oshy?"

"Huh?" Josh plunged his hands into his pockets and shook his head, trying to clear the memory of those teeth tearing into his arm. Lizzie had a worried look on her face. He grimaced and glanced at Brent, who was focused on Nova. "I'm fine," he said.

Just then, Nova snapped at Vortex. Josh cringed as Brent rushed to Nova's side. "There's also the issue of temperament."

"People temperament or dog temperament?" asked Lizzie.

"Sometimes both," said Brent, calming the dog. "When Hank left for Otter Falls, he gave me Nova. He's a bit high-strung."

Josh watched as Brent unsnapped Nova's tug line and led him back to the dog yard.

Lizzie turned toward her brother. "Are you sure you're all right, Josh?"

"I said I'm *fine*." He wished she would just drop it.

"Okay, okay. But you know you don't have to do this, right? It's okay to say no."

Josh stared at the yipping dogs. He tried to collect himself as Brent returned, dropping a heavy blanket into the sled basket.

"I'm not sure what's going on with Nova," Brent said. "Dogs have distinct personalities, and you have to respect that. But he's been acting mean lately. I'm not sure what's wrong with him."

"He's a dog," Josh muttered to Lizzie, who frowned.

Brent led Barney out to the sled. He snapped on his tug line and the rest of the neck lines.

Lizzie turned back to Brent. "It seems like a ton of work to take care of the team."

Hike!

"For sure," said Brent. "But it's all part of being a sprint racer. You might train far from home—" he pointed to the sprawling fields beyond the barn "—and it's your dogs who will get you back home alive."

Josh shivered despite his heavy parka.

"Can we get in the sled?" Lizzie asked.

"Almost." Brent held up two pieces of fabric that looked like socks.

"I don't need another pair," said Lizzie. "My feet are the one part of me that is warm."

"These booties are for the dogs," explained Brent. "They protect their feet just like boots do for us. Snow and ice can be abrasive and get stuck between the toes and around the pad of the paw. It can turn into a painful ice ball. Like having a rock in your shoe. Each dog needs two pairs. One for the front paws and one for the back."

As soon as the dogs had on their booties, Josh and Lizzie lowered their goggles over their eyes and climbed into the sled. Lizzie pulled the blanket up around them.

Brent got behind and stood on the rear section of the runners. His hands gripped the handlebar of the sled. "You guys ready?" he cried, the dogs still howling in anticipation.

"Let's go for it!" Lizzie said.

"Hike!" cried Brent.

Instantly silent, the team bounded across the snowy field.

"It's so quiet," Josh said.

"They're only focused on the run," explained Brent.

"This is more fun than skiing!" Lizzie cried.

Snug in the sled and covered with a blanket, they sped toward a trail bordered by snow-covered pine trees. The sled made a *whoosh* as it cut through the newly fallen snow. The trail narrowed, and several times Josh thought the dogs might careen into a tree. But each time, they moved easily around the curves as Brent directed them.

Lizzie took out her phone to capture a video, but some of the snow kicked up from the running dogs sprayed into the sled. "Yikes, better not film right now."

She turned to look at Josh. "Knock, knock!"

"Who's there?" asked Josh.

"Dog."

"Dog what?"

"Doggone it! This is fun. Don't you think, Oshy?"

Josh's face was blank, but then he managed a half-grin. "It's all right, I guess."

They pulled into a large clearing. When Brent applied the brake and cried, *"Whoa!"* the dogs slowed to a stop. Brent stepped off the runners and walked around to the front of the sled. "Either of you want a turn?"

Josh hunched his shoulders as he sank lower in the sled. *No way*. If he could have disappeared, he would have.

Hike!

Lizzie's eyes danced with excitement. "I was hoping you would ask!" she said, throwing off the blanket. "I stand on the runners, right?"

"Yes. Put both hands on the handlebar."

Lizzie got into position.

Brent moved behind her and stepped on the runners. "You know how to start the team?"

"*Hike!*" she yelled in reply.

The sled dog team took off like a rocket, tearing across the field of snow.

"Woooo! I love this!" cried Lizzie. She held on tight to the handlebar as the team bounded forward.

The whipping wind stung the small area of Josh's face not covered by his hood.

Soon, the billowing red flag atop the Parkerview silo was in sight. As they got closer to home, Lizzie yelled, "*Whoa!*" and the dogs came to a stop.

Lizzie turned to Brent as she stepped off the runners. "Can you take it from here? I don't want them running into the barn."

"No danger of that. Sometimes I think they know the trail better than I do. But I can take over." Brent gave her a big smile. "You did great!"

"Thanks." Lizzie elbowed her brother. "See? Nothing to it."

Josh's heart raced at the thought. *Maybe to her. Not to me.*

Chapter 5
A Mean Shadow

Once they reached the barn, Lizzie carried the blanket inside while Josh unpacked the rest of the sled.

Brent was busy unsnapping the lines and tethering the dogs in the dog yard. He paused next to Popsicle. "How're you doing, girl?" Brent watched her move around her house.

"Is she limping?" Josh asked.

"You spotted that too?" said Brent. "Good eye!"

Grateful for Brent's compliment, Josh allowed a small smile. He hoped Popsicle would be all right.

"She'll walk evenly and then seem to favor her left side," Brent went on. "I'll have to monitor her."

A Mean Shadow

After all the dogs were in the dog yard, Brent gave them treats. The dogs gulped down the food and sniffed for more. From the safety of the other side of the fence, Josh watched them.

Just then, Aunt Terry poked her head out the side door. "Those rolls are ready whenever you are."

"Thanks, Mom." Brent followed her inside.

Lizzie moved closer to Josh. "The dogs are beautiful, aren't they?"

Josh had to admit they were. "Yes. At a safe distance." He patted the fence.

The twins stared across the fields. A shadowy figure on a distant hill seemed to be pulling a dog on a leash and shouting.

"It must be hard to train a sled dog," said Lizzie.

Josh laughed. "I read that some trainers live in the kennels with their dogs. Imagine curled up next to *dogs*."

As they watched, the twins saw the man's hand come down on the back end of the dog. Then an angry voice boomed across the field. A sharp yelp echoed in the still air.

Josh stopped laughing. "They're sure not my best friends," he said quietly. "But they shouldn't be hit."

Brent came out of the house carrying a tray. He glanced at his watch. "We'd better get going. The race qualification dinner meeting starts in thirty minutes, and I've got to get these rolls to the community hall kitchen."

ADVENTURE USA

They walked down the driveway and climbed into the truck.

"Someone over there is really mad at his dog," Josh said.

"Where?" Brent stared across the field.

There was no one in sight.

"He was yelling—" Josh looked at Brent. "Then he hit the dog."

"That's terrible." Brent pursed his lips. "Some people feel the more you yell, the more the dogs understand. But it's the opposite. The more you yell, the less they trust you."

Brent drove carefully along the snow-packed roads. A forest of pine trees stretched into the distance. Several houses dotted the landscape. Soon, they reached the small town of Hawk River, east of Wasilla.

"I see a bank, a post office, and a traffic light," said Lizzie. "Is that it?"

"Hawk River has a few more businesses," said Brent. "But it's a small town. Most people shop in Palmer down the road about ten miles."

They passed several churches and a combined elementary/high school. Beyond the school was a sign for Hawk River Community Center.

Brent pulled into the parking lot and grabbed the rolls from the back as the twins got out.

Inside the community center, the warmth hit them as the cold had earlier. Brent stopped at the front table. His friend,

A Mean Shadow

Will Meetik, had a list in front of him. He was marking off names as people checked in.

"Hey, buddy!" Brent said.

Will looked up. "Hey, Brent. How are you doing?"

"My times are up and down. Not as fast as I'd like."

"Same with me. And my dad has big expectations for me."

"That's a bit of pressure."

Will nodded. "Yep."

Next to the table was a large wooden sign listing the rules set forth by the Association.

Josh elbowed Lizzie. "Look at number 4."

"*Whips are forbidden,*" read Lizzie, "*on and off the race trail.*" Her eyes got wide. "I hope they enforce that."

Josh could feel his jaw tighten. "I hope so too."

Brent led them into the main room where long tables were set up for dinner. He handed the rolls he'd brought to one of the servers. Photographs of mushers decorated the walls. Brent pointed to one of them. "That's a picture of my friend Will with his dad, taken two years ago."

"*First place winner,*" read Lizzie. "Wow."

Josh took a deep breath. The delicious smell of dinner filled the air. "I'm starving."

Lizzie rolled her eyes. "So what else is new?"

"This time I'm really starving." Josh stood on tiptoe to scout out the serving table. "All that cold air."

"All that breakfast and lunch should have filled you up," added Lizzie.

"That was hours ago," said Josh.

Josh and Lizzie followed Brent toward the serving line. Atasak was first in line.

"How's your dad?" one server asked her.

Atasak let out a deep sigh. "Not so good. The recovery is going to be longer than we thought."

"Come around to the kitchen after the meeting," the server said. "We always have leftovers. You can take some home."

"Really?" Atasak said. "Thank you so much."

Across the room, a tall man with a beard and broad shoulders raised a massive hand and waved. He hurried over and shook Brent's hand. He was the same man who had stopped by Parkerview Farm to ask about dog food.

"Hey, Hank!" Brent said. "I haven't introduced you to my cousins, Josh and Lizzie. Hank lives on the next farm, just over the ridge from Parkerview. We were in school together until he graduated last year."

After saying hello, the twins grabbed their trays and started through the line.

"I think Hank is the guy in the field," whispered Josh.

Lizzie turned around for a second look. "No. That man was heavier and taller."

"Sure. He had on a thick parka and a large hat." Josh couldn't resist wolfing down half a hot dog. "And we know he's got a temper."

"But why would an owner mistreat his dog?" asked Lizzie. "That doesn't teach the dog anything." She took another look. "I don't think it's him. That other guy might have had on glasses too."

"I think it's the same person." Josh held out his fist. "Bet?"

"For what?"

"A chocolate peanut butter cup. Aunt Terry has a stash."

Lizzie tapped Josh's fist. "You're on."

Chapter 6

Hank

Josh snatched two more hot dogs, baked beans, sauerkraut, French fries, a brownie, and the second-to-last sugar cookie.

"Why don't you ask for a larger tray?" said Lizzie. "Or get a cart to deliver that load of food to the table?"

"He's got the right idea," said Brent, coming up behind them. "The desserts always go fast at these dinners. Especially Hank's brownies."

"You made these?" Josh asked.

"Sure did. I try to help." Hank laughed. "It's my grandmother's recipe. Messy Bessies she calls them. It's been in the family for years."

Hank

"He brings them to the races, and they sell out every time," added Brent.

"Someday I'm going to sell them around the world!" Hank cried. "Make a million dollars!"

With that, Josh grabbed another brownie.

Lizzie chose lasagna and a salad. She put two cookies on her tray. The twins followed Brent and Hank to a table. The room was filling up. Brent put down his tray, and Josh sat opposite him.

Hank slid into the seat next to Josh. "I hear you've got a problem with dogs."

Josh felt his face burn.

"Not really." Brent reached for the ketchup. "He just needs a little time."

"You get nipped?" Hank continued.

Josh was stone-faced.

Hank pushed up the sleeve of his sweater. Red scars crisscrossed his arm. "That's part of life."

Josh pulled back, horrified. He squeezed ketchup on his hot dogs. *Not of my life*, he thought.

"Battle scars." Hank snickered and clamped his hand on Josh's shoulder. "Means you're a real soldier."

"Not interested in that army," Josh said in a quiet voice. He reached for the mustard and relish.

"Don't let them know it," Hank went on. "A dog who smells your fear—"

"Easy," Brent interrupted. "You're making it sound worse than it is."

Changing the subject, Lizzie peered at Josh's plate. "Is there really a hot dog in there?"

"I don't know." Josh smashed the food with his fork. "Let me find out."

"Yuck!" cried Lizzie. "Just eat it."

Josh devoured one hot dog in several bites. In minutes, the rest of his food was nearly gone. Looking across the table, he eyed Lizzie's tray with interest. "How's that lasagna of yours?" His fork hovered above her plate like a fighter jet. "Want to split it?"

"No way," said Lizzie. "And if you dare go back for more, I'm calling the food police on you."

A police officer stopped at their table.

"Looks like you don't have to call anyone, Lizzie," said Hank.

Lizzie's face turned beet red.

"Guys, this is Officer Nelson," said Brent. "Part-time police officer and veterinarian."

"That's a small town for you. You've got to wear lots of hats," said Officer Nelson. "How's everyone doing?"

"Good," said Lizzie.

"Great," said Brent.

"Couldn't be better," said Hank.

"I hear you're a favorite to win," Officer Nelson said to

Hank

Brent. "They say you have it in the bag."

"I think I have a good shot at it," he said. "If my dogs stay well."

"I remember last year." Officer Nelson frowned. "You had to drop two dogs."

"One came down with a virus, and the other one hit an ice patch coming off a curve." Brent paused, remembering the moment. "It was terrible."

"Let's hope this year is much better." Officer Nelson turned to Hank. "Are you getting ready to race?"

"Not just race," said Hank. "I'm getting ready to win."

"Uh-uh," kidded Brent. "That prize money's all mine."

Hank banged his fist on the table. Startled, Josh flinched. "Nope. That money's got my name on it. It's *got* to be mine. Got to fix up my jeep. No jeep, no job."

"How are your dogs, Hank?" Officer Nelson asked. "Is Heidi still limping?"

"She's great," said Hank. "Couldn't be better. She's got a tight tug all the way."

"That means she's a good puller," Josh told Lizzie as he finished eating his brownies.

Hank let out a cackle. "Hey! Do you think you're an expert or something?"

Josh felt his face get hot again. "I like to read."

Hank leaned close to Josh and glared. "That's fine, but

don't dare confuse book learning with life learning. That's what separates men from boys."

Josh stared at his plate. It was true. He'd never be a man like Brent.

"Hank, keep an eye on Heidi," said Brent. "I thought she was limping at the end of the last race."

Hank finished his hamburger. "Maybe a loose bootie, that's all."

Officer Nelson waved and headed for the back of the room.

People at other tables were busy cleaning up. Josh and Lizzie picked up their trays and went to the dish room.

"That man in the field was him," whispered Josh. "The dog he smacked was probably Heidi. Pay up time, Lizard."

"Perhaps," she said. "But why would a musher want to hurt his dogs?"

"Maybe the only thing he cares about is winning," Josh said.

In the front of the room, a woman had moved to the microphone. Josh and Lizzie listened as she explained the rules of the upcoming practice sprint. Each participant had to have time on the trail before the county finals to ensure that only experienced mushers competed.

"Saturday's trail is short. Less than an hour," said Brent. "Most of us will finish before that. I'm trying to break forty minutes. Afterward, they'll use our times to give us starting

Hank

positions for the big county finals race."

"It also gives you an idea who you have to beat," said Hank. "Since everyone's time is posted, you know who's the fastest."

"I guess the two of you like racing against each other," said Lizzie.

"We've never competed together," said Brent. "Hank got me started years ago. Then his family moved to Otter Falls. He raced with the Fairbanks team. Two months ago, he moved back. This is his first race down here."

"My first money race too," said Hank. "In Fairbanks, you raced for points, which could earn you a trophy at the end of the season."

Brent put his hand on Hank's shoulder. "This race is tough because the first prize winner is the only one who gets the money. The other winners just get trophies."

"Keep mushing," said the woman at the microphone. "Put in your time, and we'll see you all on Saturday."

Brent and Hank went forward to sign up for the qualifying sprint. Lizzie took a thick napkin out of her pocket.

"What's in there?" Josh wanted to know.

"Something yummy," Lizzie said.

"Oh, man," said Josh. "You're going to sit in front of me and not share?"

"Not a big snack," said Lizzie. "Just a little one, Oshy."

Josh eyed Lizzie's fingers as she unwrapped her napkin.

Inside was a sugar cookie. He could feel his mouth watering.

"How about a taste, Lizard?" he asked.

"Sure. For a bet." Lizzie picked up the cookie and broke it in half. "How about a dog bet?"

Josh curled his lip. "I'm not barking like a dog for a cookie."

"Not what I was thinking."

"I'm not wagging my tail either," said Josh.

"You don't have to act like a dog."

"Then..." Josh stared at his sister. "No way, Lizard. I'm not stupid."

"Just pet a dog. For like a minute."

"You heard what Brent said about Nova," Josh growled. "He's 'temperamental.' That's a nice way of saying he'll snap you in half in a second."

"Before we leave Alaska, I bet you'll be a dog liker." Lizzie smiled. "Two of those peanut butter cups say you will."

"You're on," Josh said as they bumped their fists together. Secretly, Josh hoped it was possible. Being a dog liker would mean a lot to Brent.

Lizzie handed over half of the cookie.

Josh devoured it in one gulp. "Thanks!"

Back home, Josh and Lizzie went inside while Brent checked the dog yard. Lizzie rushed to join Aunt Terry and Uncle Bob as they sat by the fire. Josh flopped on the couch.

Just then the landline phone rang.

Uncle Bob picked it up. "Hello, you two!" he said. "They're right here. Just got back from the race meeting," he added.

"It's Mom and Dad!" cried Lizzie, jumping up. "Let me talk!" Uncle Bob handed her the cordless phone.

Josh slumped into the couch, feeling his face get warm. He hoped she wouldn't share that Vortex disaster in front of everyone.

"It's been amazing," Lizzie said as she wandered into the kitchen. "I got to…" Her voice faded off.

Brent came in from the hall and lifted Trivial Pursuit down from the bookshelf. "How about the men against the women? Dad can be the moderator to keep the teams even."

"Sure," said Josh.

Aunt Terry cleared off the coffee table, and they began setting up the game. Uncle Bob read off some cards, and they took turns answering.

Soon Lizzie came back into the room. "You want to say hi?" she asked, handing Josh the phone.

Josh's hand was clammy as he took it. "Hey," he said, moving toward the hall in case some embarrassing questions came up.

"Just checking in," said Dad.

"We know you're in good hands with Aunt Terry and Uncle Bob," said his mother.

They chatted about their research, hiking on a glacier, the twins' assignments, and Brent's upcoming county finals race.

"We're hoping to finish up by then," said Mom.

"It's been hard to call since we've been mostly in the backcountry," added Dad.

"But everything is going okay?" Mom asked.

"The snow's been awesome," Josh said without hesitating. "And Brent and I are about to challenge Aunt Terry and Lizzie to a game of Trivial Pursuit."

"Ha!" said Dad. "That should be quite the match. May the best man win."

"Now wait a second," Mom started.

In a few minutes they said goodbye, and Josh disconnected the call with a sigh of relief. The last thing he needed was a reminder of how he'd made a fool of himself.

"We're going to thrash you," said Lizzie as Josh sat down to play. "Aunt Terry does crosswords. She's the champ of trivia."

"Wrong," said Josh. "You've forgotten that Brent's team won the high school Quiz Bowl three years in a row."

Several hours later, the men had won, and Josh couldn't help hooting.

"You guys got lucky," said Lizzie. "We demand a rematch."

"Any time," said Josh. "It will give you a chance to memorize Wikipedia."

In the middle of the night, Josh awoke with a start. He heard dogs barking. Getting out of bed, he peered through the window. The bright light of the full moon illuminated the peaceful scene, but shadows from the thin branches gave the dog yard an eerie appearance.

Suddenly, a movement near the driveway caught Josh's eye. Was someone there?

Josh blinked and looked again. He thought he'd glimpsed something like a tall shadow, but he wasn't sure. Was it a deer looking for food? Or a person? He remained at the window, searching, before finally returning to bed.

CHAPTER 7
The Sprint

The Parker family was up early on Saturday for the Big Lake qualifying sprint. Uncle Bob fixed a huge breakfast of pancakes, waffles, eggs, bacon, sausage, and fruit.

Josh reached for his fifth pancake and drizzled syrup on top.

"We can't make maple syrup up here," Uncle Bob said. "No sugar maples. But in late April or early May, the birch tree sap starts flowing. We tap into that. It's a good substitute." He motioned toward the pitcher. "Don't you think?"

"It's awesome," Josh said. "Tastes the same to me."

Brent turned away from the window. "It's a balmy 30 degrees. But that wind chill will probably make it feel like 20 degrees or lower."

The Sprint

"I put out some tops and bottoms along with socks on the chest in the hallway," said Aunt Terry. "Take whatever you need."

"We'll need to layer up," Brent added. "Woolen long underwear, base layer, fleece, maybe a vest, and a parka."

"Brent's right. Layers are the best choice," Aunt Terry continued. "Being too hot can be almost as bad as being too cold. You don't want to sweat."

The twins helped clear the table and then went upstairs where they chose the warm clothes they'd need for the arctic weather.

Later, Lizzie was first down the stairs. She slid into a chair by the jigsaw puzzle.

"I'm going to finish that cloud on the top left," she said, scanning some nearby pieces.

Josh was right behind her. "What about the English essay? It's due this week."

"Done," said Lizzie. "What about yours?"

"Done," said Josh. "And sent."

"Did you check out Mom's blog?" Lizzie asked. "They're hiking another glacier."

"Looked pretty cool—literally."

"Ha ha," said Lizzie. "And that dog yard they visited is just like Brent's."

Josh had skimmed over that post, not needing another reminder. "And by the way," he started, "I hope you didn't—"

"Hey, you two," Uncle Bob interrupted, holding up a large pocket watch on a cord. "Who wants to be our timer for the race?"

"I do!" called Lizzie.

"This watch has been in the family for years. We use it for all the races." Uncle Bob handed it to her. "Very simple to operate. It times in seconds. Push the top button down to start. Then push it down again to stop."

Lizzie looped the cord over her head. "Now I'm official! Let's see how long we take to get ready," she added as she set it.

As Brent grabbed his parka, Uncle Bob held up a cooler. "We've got the sandwiches in case anyone's hungry after the sprint."

"Salmon salad," Aunt Terry said. "A certain musher's favorite."

"Thanks, Mom and Dad," called Brent. "I'll get the dogs ready to get in the truck."

"Come on!" Lizzie elbowed Josh. "Let's go see how it's done."

"You can't get enough of those dogs, can you?"

"I am curious."

"Well, I'm not."

Lizzie headed for the mudroom. "See you later then."

As Josh watched Lizzie run outside to where Brent was attaching the dog box to the truck bed, he suddenly feared he'd

The Sprint

miss out on something. He pulled on his parka and Phillies hat and bolted outside.

"This is an eight-holer," Brent was saying to Lizzie. "There are spaces in this box for four dogs on each side. I spread straw or wood chips in each compartment."

Josh hesitated, then pushed himself forward. Midnight placed her paws on the side of the truck. Then Brent picked up her hind legs and loaded her into a compartment.

"Popsicle still seems to favor her left side." Brent was thoughtful. "I've switched her out for Sassy. I wanted to give her sprinting experience, but I think rest is what she needs."

Once all the dogs were loaded and the doors were securely closed, Brent moved the sprinting sled closer to the truck. Inside the netting, he placed an axe, snowshoes, and a large bag of extra booties along with a backpack.

Josh moved closer now that the dogs were in the dog box. "Do you need all that extra equipment for a short sprint?"

"Probably not," said Brent. "But I always bring the necessities. Anything could happen at any time, and racers must be prepared. For themselves and their dogs."

Brent zipped up the sled bag, hoisted the sled on top of the dog box, and carefully tied it down.

Aunt Terry and Uncle Bob came out, and they all piled into the truck.

Lizzie clicked the stopwatch. "Fifteen minutes, thirty-five seconds. Not bad."

Aunt Terry laughed. "Maybe we set a new record for getting ready."

"We'll take the Parks Highway," explained Uncle Bob as he turned right out of the long driveway. "That's the primary route between Anchorage and Fairbanks. The Alaska Railroad runs parallel to it."

The narrow road snaked through the forest. Snow drifts towered beside nearby guard rails.

After passing through the town of Wasilla, Uncle Bob turned left on Big Lake Road. "When Aunt Terry and I first got married, we lived in Kenai. I had a Cessna 206 and flew tourists out here to fish."

The Sprint

Aunt Terry smiled. "He'd get some for us too. Delicious rainbow trout, Arctic char, and northern pike."

Soon, they pulled into the Blue Lake Recreation Area parking lot. Other trucks with trailers or dog boxes behind the cabs had already arrived. Uncle Bob parked near a staging area, and Brent hurried to the registration tent. When he emerged, he was wearing a Tyvek bib with 00923 written on it. Atasak was right behind him.

"Great day for the qualifying sprint," she said.

Brent nodded. "Good luck!"

"You too," she said, heading across the parking lot.

Lizzie took her phone out of her pocket and filmed a quick clip of the scene.

Brent got right to work. He lifted the sled off the top of the dog box, laid out the gangline, and got ready to hook up the dogs.

Other sprint racers were organizing their equipment. The chilly air was alive with the raucous yips and howling of the dog teams.

Josh stood near the truck.

"They're *harnessed*," Lizzie whispered to him.

"I *know* that."

"Hey, Brent!" called a voice from across the parking lot.

"Hank!" cried Brent.

"Ready to go?"

Brent tapped his handlebar. "Sure am. Hope to break forty minutes."

Hank let out a loud snicker. "I plan to break thirty-five!"

"He sure is competitive," said Josh to Lizzie.

"Of course," she said. "He wants the prize money at the county finals."

"By the way, did you hear the dogs barking in the middle of the night?" asked Josh.

"Nope," she said. "I was asleep."

"They woke me up," he said. "Then I thought I saw something near the dog yard. Or someone."

Lizzie frowned. "Don't start. No one sane is wandering around in the middle of the night."

I didn't say he was sane, thought Josh.

Josh watched as Brent and Hank moved to the starting line. Hank's sled basket was partly uncovered. A black handle stuck out from underneath the sled bag.

"Look at Hank's sled!" Josh whispered.

Lizzie moved so she had a better look. "I don't see anything."

"That black handle."

"You're too suspicious. It's an *axe* handle."

"It could be a whip," said Josh.

"That's against the rules. He'd be disqualified."

"Maybe he's *desperate!*"

The twins turned back to the starting line. Ready to run, the sled dogs shrieked and howled with excitement. Each mushing

The Sprint

team lined up in order of their starting time. They would race against the clock, not directly against each other. Lizzie had the stopwatch in her hand, ready to set it.

Suddenly, it was Brent's turn. He called, "*Hike!*" to his team, and they tore down the trail.

Several other mushers sped out from the starting line, leaving at two-minute intervals.

Soon, they saw a musher in a silver-and-black parka approach the starting gate.

"There's Atasak," said Lizzie.

They watched as she got into position and then sped off into the distance.

Finally, it was Hank's turn.

"Hank looks angry," said Josh.

"Determined, if you ask me," said Lizzie. "Maybe he's mad that Brent went first. But it doesn't matter. Everyone's timed."

The day was sunny, but the air was crisp and cold. The thermometer on the starting line shed said twenty degrees.

"I'm glad I wore layers," said Lizzie. "Double socks, double mittens, double woolen tops."

Josh stuck his mittened hands into his parka pockets and stamped his feet. "My feet feel like bricks. These boots are warm, but I should have added those mukluk liners."

"My nose feels like an icicle." Lizzie breathed deeply. "And my nose hairs might be frozen."

"That usually doesn't happen until minus ten or below," Josh said.

"You and your details," said Lizzie as she pulled her neck gaiter up over her nose and ears. "But you're probably right."

"Let's walk over to the finish line," said Aunt Terry. "What's Brent's time so far?"

Lizzie pulled the stopwatch out of her parka. "Twenty-nine minutes, forty-five seconds."

"I hope he can make the time he wants," Uncle Bob said.

"Me too." Josh tightened his hood. "Hank sure is confident."

"He was brash as a kid too," Aunt Terry said.

Uncle Bob glanced back at the starting line. "He's older now, though. Should have outgrown it."

A small crowd had gathered behind the orange fencing at the finish line. Timing officials stood nearby. One by one, a few mushers whizzed over the finish line.

Josh and Lizzie, along with their aunt and uncle, stood off to the side. Lizzie checked the time again. "Thirty-eight minutes, forty-five seconds."

Uncle Bob's eyes twinkled. "He's close."

Suddenly, they saw a familiar red parka.

"Go, Brent, go!" they cried. "Go!"

There was a *whoosh*, and Brent yelled, "*Whoa!*" as he sped past.

The Sprint

"Forty-one minutes, fifteen seconds!" called a timing official.

Josh and Lizzie jumped up and down screaming, "Hooray for Brent!"

Josh thought Brent looked disappointed as he slowed the team. But he moved along the gangline encouraging each dog. "Good boy! Great job, Thunder! Super girl, Midnight!"

"I know you wanted to be under forty minutes," said Josh. "But you were close."

Brent sighed. "I'm pleased but a little worried. Sassy isn't as experienced as Popsicle. I sure hope I can put her back in the lineup."

Just then Atasak sailed over the finish line.

"Forty-two minutes, fifty seconds!" called another timing official.

Atasak shook her head as she slowed her team. "I got hung up on one of the turns. Lost precious seconds there."

"It's still a good time," said Brent.

"Maybe. But is it good enough to win the finals?" Atasak pursed her lips as she moved out of the way with her dog team.

Several other mushers sped over the finish line. Then Lizzie spotted Hank's yellow parka. "Here comes Hank."

"Forty-four minutes, twenty seconds!" came the call.

Hank's face was flushed, and he wore a deep frown.

"This sprint was worthless," he said with disgust.

"At least we both finished," said Brent. "We'll still qualify for the finals." He put his hand on Hank's shoulder. "I'm above my time too. Sassy's acting—"

"They're all acting up," Hank snarled.

He narrowed his eyes, fury blanketing his face. Gazing back at his team, he muttered, "Time to change up the training."

Josh met Lizzie's gaze.

Time to use the—

He couldn't even bear to think about it.

Chapter 8

Popsicle

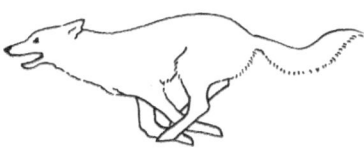

The next morning, Josh found himself up early. His feet had felt like ice cubes yesterday, so he knew he had to dress warmer. Downstairs in the hall closet, he pulled out a bin of liners. He found a pair about his size and stuffed them in his boots. Grabbing his parka, hat, and gloves, he went outside. Once again, the cold hit him like a slap. More snow had fallen overnight. He was grateful for his warm footwear as he tramped along the path.

Josh made his way toward the barn. The sun was coming up, and the sky was a deep pink. He had planned to take a hike through the back fields. But instead, he was peering through the fence at the dogs.

Earlier, when he'd looked out the window, it had been almost impossible to see the dog yard in the blizzard. The wind had been even more menacing, and the snow seemed to fall sideways. Now the dogs were waking up too. They stretched and shook their fur.

Popsicle walked closer to the fence and sniffed the ground. Josh knew he was safe, but sweat broke out on his forehead, and his mouth felt dry.

He edged closer. He could see how she favored one side over the other. She let out a sharp yip, turned around, and sat. What was causing her pain? He bent over to see better, feeling for the flashlight and magnifying glass he carried in his pocket for emergencies.

Who was he kidding? He'd never get that close to a dog.

Suddenly, a truck roared up the driveway and then came to a stop. An older man stuck his head out the window.

"I got the dog food," he yelled. "Where do you want it?"

"Brent stores it in the barn," Josh said.

The truck driver pulled into a small parking area.

"Hey, snowman!" called Lizzie.

Josh turned around to see her heading toward him holding a mug.

"Want some hot chocolate?"

Josh eagerly took a sip. The cocoa tasted delicious.

Lizzie took a carrot out of her pocket. "Hold this in your mouth, and you'll look just like a snowman."

Popsicle

"Ha ha," said Josh. He brushed the snow off his jacket. "It was really coming down earlier."

The truck driver came out of the barn and walked toward them. "Owen" was printed on his jacket.

"They think a blizzard's coming," Owen said. "Stay close to home." He handed Josh the receipt. "By the way, how long has Hank Fitzgerald been back? I just delivered food to his place."

"A couple of months, according to Brent," Lizzie said.

"I didn't know he was back to mushing."

"He qualified yesterday for the county finals," said Josh.

"I thought they put him on probation," Owen said.

"Probation?" Josh sputtered. "For what?"

"Not sure of the details."

"That's serious, isn't it?"

Owen nodded. "For some infractions, it's automatic."

Josh wondered exactly *which* infractions would trigger probation.

Owen opened the door of the truck. "How's Nova?"

"Brent had to take him out of the team the other day," Lizzie said. "He was fighting with Vortex."

"That's a real shame," Owen said. "Disrupts the social structure. Can make the other dogs compete for that place."

Owen glanced at the dog yard. "Nova was one of Hank's dogs, I think. Brent might want to watch him."

"He was just acting grumpy," said Lizzie. "Maybe it's no big deal."

"Dogs don't act up without a reason." Owen shoved his hands in his pockets. "I hope Brent figures it out. I know he's counting on winning to get money for college."

Lizzie watched as Owen drove off. "I guess sled dogs are supposed to get along. But Nova's just being a dog."

"Exactly the problem. Nova has it in his head that he doesn't like something, so he snaps at it." Josh frowned. "They're *dogs*. And I don't trust them."

Just then, Atasak rushed up from the other side of the barn. "Where's Brent?"

"He's inside," said Lizzie. "What's wrong?"

"It's Nova!" Atasak cried. "He's growling and lunging at Vortex."

"I'll get him!" Lizzie ran for the house.

Josh turned to Atasak. "Maybe he's having a bad day."

Atasak let out a long breath. "You don't understand dogs, do you?"

"I understand this—dogs bite. One bit me."

"Most dogs aren't like that." Atasak put down the bucket she was carrying. "Did you ever fall off your bike?"

Josh shrugged. "Sure. What does that have to do with dogs?"

"Did you get back on?"

Popsicle

"Of course, I did. So what?"

"That's what you need to do now," Atasak said softly. "Get back on."

"Dogs bite," said Josh. "Bikes don't. Simple as that."

Brent flew out of the house with Lizzie. He dashed across the driveway.

"Is Vortex all right?" he asked Atasak.

"She's fine. She growled back." Atasak picked up the bucket. "But I don't like it."

"I don't either. Nova came from Hank's team. He should know better." Brent's face was twisted with worry. "A dog like Nova can ruin a team."

"Do you think Hank is harder on his team?" Josh asked carefully. "Is that why Nova's fighting?"

"Owen stopped by with the dog food," Lizzie began. "He mentioned Hank was—" she swallowed "—on probation?"

"That's a big misunderstanding," Brent said. "I've known Hank for years."

"Is he still on probation?" Josh wondered.

"No!" said Brent sharply. "There's a lot of competition in Fairbanks. Some new mushers were making assumptions. I better check on Nova." Brent followed Atasak into the dog yard.

Josh glanced at Lizzie. She looked as worried as he felt.

Nova could disrupt the team and ruin any chance for Brent to win the county finals.

Chapter 9
Dr. Josh

After lunch, Josh cleared the table and wiped off the placemats in the dining room. Pictures of Brent and his dogs covered one wall.

There's not one picture of him alone, thought Josh. *He's hugging his dogs in every picture. He's not afraid. Why do I have to be?*

Josh picked up one of the trophies on the chest near the window. "CHALLENGE RACE—FIRST PLACE" was engraved beneath a running dog. He put down the trophy and picked up one with two dogs straining in a harness. That one said, "MOST IMPROVED MUSHER." The date was just two years ago.

Josh sighed with disgust as he pushed in the chairs. *If Brent can do it, why can't I?*

Dr. Josh

With a final glance at a row of hooks holding medals, he left the room and tossed the towel in the dish drainer.

Brent came through the back door carrying logs for the fireplace. "Do you want to go trailblazing?"

With or without the dogs? thought Josh.

"Just the three of us," Brent added, as though reading Josh's mind. "I was going to try a new trail later, and sometimes I walk it first."

"Sure." Josh loved being outside in the snow.

The twins suited up in their snow gear and followed Brent to the barn. He stopped outside the dog yard. As he did, Popsicle came up to the fence. She sniffed Brent and wagged her tail.

"I don't get it," said Brent. "She's still limping."

Popsicle whined a little and tried to put her nose through the fence.

"There she goes again!" Brent cried. "She whined last night, too, when she circled the ground to lie down."

Josh stepped forward slightly. "Have you checked her foot pad?"

"That's the first thing I did," Brent said. "But there doesn't seem to be anything wrong."

"That book I was reading talked about razor snow—" Josh began.

Brent nodded. "Snow so sharp it can cut the foot pads. I checked her pads. Several times."

"The book says—" Josh continued.

"You and your books," interrupted Lizzie. "But seriously, Brent. He's usually right."

"Sometimes the cuts are tiny, and fur covers them," Josh went on. "They can be almost impossible to see. There was a picture of them. They looked very painful."

"Well then, Dr. Josh, let's take a look." Brent went into the dog yard and carried out Popsicle.

Backing up, Josh felt for the magnifying glass in his pocket and held it out for Brent. "See what you think."

"Oh, no you don't. You saw the picture. You know what they look like." Brent held up Popsicle's paw. "The doctor's got to examine the patient."

Me and my big mouth, thought Josh. At least Brent had Popsicle in a bear hug. He inched closer.

Josh had a death grip on the magnifying glass. "Move the fur back around the right edge of the paw," he said, picking up a twig as a pointer.

Brent did as he was told, and Popsicle let out a shrill whimper.

"There it is!" With the twig, Josh pointed to an area under the fur. He positioned the magnifying glass so Brent could see. "It's hard to find. Can you see it?"

Brent moved Popsicle's paw closer to the magnifier. "I can now. It must have been extremely painful for her. Like having a blister on your toe and running a marathon in bare feet." He smiled. "Nice job, Josh. Thanks."

Josh felt his cheeks grow warm at the compliment.

Brent gestured with his head. "Lizzie, get my sled pack. It's hanging by the door. I've got medication in there."

Lizzie found the bag and brought it out. Josh waited awkwardly.

"The tubes are in the side compartment," added Brent. "A little dab on a swab should do it."

Lizzie squeezed some medicine on the swab and handed it to Brent.

"Not me, Lizzie," Brent said. "I've got to hold her." He turned to Josh. "You're going to have to do it, Doctor."

Josh's face broke out in a sweat despite the freezing air. "Me? I—" he started.

"Yes, you!" Brent cried. "Popsicle's in pain, and we've got to help her!"

Josh knew Brent was right. He had to move, but he was frozen with fear.

"You dab it on, and I'll hold her—or the other way around," Brent said. Popsicle let out a sharp yip. "Come on! I can't hold her much longer."

Josh inched toward his cousin and the whimpering dog. His heart was hammering like a marching band. Slowly, he took the swab and touched it to the cut. Popsicle wriggled and let out another small whimper.

"Put a second dab on it, and I'll massage it in," Brent said. "The medicine numbs the area a little and then seals it so it can heal."

Josh prepared another swab and touched it to the injured paw. This time there was no sound from Popsicle.

His heart still beating at a furious tempo, Josh stepped back and watched Brent work the medicine into her footpad. Next, he wrapped it in gauze and slipped on a bootie.

"Is it usual for dogs to step in razor snow?" Josh asked.

"I've run into it a couple of times. Why?"

"The dogs woke me up the other night. I thought I saw something or someone outside."

"I'm sure you did. There are animals everywhere. Usually, the dogs don't bark, as the sounds are familiar. But sometimes it's a different animal or sound."

"It could have been a person," said Josh.

"Like who?" Brent asked. "Doing what?"

Josh shrugged, not willing to say what he really thought. *It could have been Hank. Hurting Popsicle.*

Brent put Popsicle on the ground and stood. Josh took a few steps backward.

"What? You're not going to let her thank you?" Brent asked. Popsicle vigorously wagged her tail.

Josh stood in his safety zone. "I just dabbed on a little medicine, that's all. She doesn't know that."

Dr. Josh

Brent looked deep into Josh's eyes. "That's where you're wrong, Cuz. Dogs know. They remember."

Finding some courage, Josh slowly extended his gloved hand toward Popsicle. She sniffed the glove, her tail still wagging fiercely.

Brent smiled. "Maybe next time her new friend will give her some pats."

Josh watched as Brent led Popsicle back to the dog yard. Then he glanced at Lizzie. She had her hand thrust out in front of her.

"Pay up time, Oshy." Lizzie's smile was bigger than ever. "I win!"

"Nope. All I did was play vet, and I didn't pet her," Josh said.

Lizzie frowned. "I was sure this was a win for me."

"Our visit's not over yet," Josh added. "And I have no intention of liking anything except breakfast, lunch, and dinner."

Chapter 10

Trailblazing

The trio headed over to the barn. In the back was a large walk-in closet.

"This is like a store!" cried Lizzie.

One wall was covered with hooks holding winter sporting equipment of all shapes and sizes. Brent held up a pair of shiny silver snowshoes. There was a loop on the top for a boot, and the bottom had metal spikes for traction.

"I thought snowshoes looked like tennis rackets for your feet," said Josh.

"My grandparents used that kind. But the new ones are sturdier and safer," Brent said.

"What's wrong with regular boots?" Lizzie asked.

Trailblazing

"Nothing," said Brent. "But snowshoes help to spread your weight out over a larger area. You stay on top of the snow instead of sinking into it. A lot more fun."

Brent handed snowshoes to Josh and Lizzie. "Winter's hard enough. My dad says you've got to have the best equipment. These are stainless steel, which helps to shed the snow as you walk. You'll see what I mean once we start walking the trail."

Lizzie slid on hers first and stomped outside. "Wow! Come look!"

Josh put on his snowshoes and followed her outside. "This is cool! I feel like a spaceman!"

Brent chuckled. "It won't take long before you'll feel comfortable." He picked up a backpack and slid it onto his back.

"Are you bringing a picnic?" Lizzie asked.

"Not exactly." Brent started walking toward the field. "It's my survival kit. Remember, winter can be tough. When you go out, you have to assume you might get stuck and not get right back."

"Plenty of cookies and hot chocolate, then?" Josh wondered.

"Sort of. Water, headlamp, emergency space blankets—these are super thin and trap your body heat to keep you warm. Also dried food and flares, like what I take when I'm out with the dogs."

"Two days before you arrived," Brent went on, "a backpacker got separated from his group in a blizzard on the other side of the lake. They found him just in time. He'd spent two days in a homemade shelter, and if they hadn't heard his whistle, they'd have missed him."

Josh loved the sight of the sun glistening on the snow, but he hadn't realized how dangerous Alaska could be.

"Hey!" Brent looked through his binoculars. "Looks like someone's out training."

In the distance, a team of dogs pulled a sled and a driver dressed in a yellow parka.

"Looks like Hank," Brent went on.

"Isn't the snow too deep for the dogs?" asked Josh.

"He's probably running on someone else's trail. Every trainer is different. Some think it strengthens the legs."

"We saw the list of rules posted at the community center," Lizzie said.

"They are strict about the rules," said Brent. "For example, they monitor dogs throughout the Iditarod. At each checkpoint, they can get a physical exam. If they're injured or ill, they need to be dropped from the race."

"I think I see a trainer who should be dropped," muttered Josh to Lizzie. "Someone should tie him to a sled and make him pull it through deep snow. Then he'd know how those dogs felt. Which means you need to hand over the peanut butter cup, Lizard. That man we saw across the field hitting his dog *was* Hank."

"Not so fast," Lizzie said. "You're talking more and more like a dog *lover*."

Trailblazing

"No way," said Josh. "I just hate to see any living thing hurt."

Brent came up next to Josh. "You want to lead?"

"Sure. What do I do?"

"Walk. Straight ahead."

Josh started walking. He felt like an explorer setting off into the great unknown. On the left and right were distant forests, but straight ahead was pure white. There were no tracks, only fresh powder from last night's storm.

Josh got into an easy stride. The air was crisp, and the wind nipped at his cheeks. Light snow danced in the air. Some parts of Alaska were feeling almost perfect.

CHAPTER 11
Snapping to the Gangline

The next morning, Hank was sitting by the fireplace when Josh came downstairs.

"Thanks for bringing over those Messie Bessies, Hank," Aunt Terry said. She and Lizzie were sorting through a large box of yarn and needles.

"I had a trayful of extras," said Hank. "And I know they're your favorite."

Josh went to the table and picked up a brownie.

"Have any nightmares last night?" Hank asked Josh. "Maybe a dream about an evil vet with a kennel full of biters?"

Josh turned his back to Hank, his face turning red with anger.

Snapping to the Gangline

Brent held up his hand. "Easy now. If you'd been bitten—"

Hank pushed up his sleeve. "I was; you were; we all have been—"

"I mean bitten, not nipped," said Brent.

Hank scowled and looked back at Josh. "You've got to toughen up, boy!" He zipped up his parka and headed for the door. Just before opening it, he stopped and turned to Brent. "See you later, buddy?"

Brent glanced at his friend. "Sure. What time?"

"Two o'clock at the Delaney Cabin." Hank had his hand on the doorknob. "I'll head out after lunch."

The arctic air jumped in as the door opened and closed. Josh felt the draft clear across the room. "What's up?" he asked his cousin.

"Hank wants to run up the North Trail near Takuta Lake and back this afternoon," said Brent. "It'll be a good training run. New to me and the dogs. There's a cabin near the lake where we can meet. You guys interested in coming?"

"We're about done with Denali over there." Lizzie gestured at the puzzle. "I'm ahead with that extra credit report and was going to get a lesson in knitting." She turned to Aunt Terry. "Can I have a rain check?" She paused. "Or a snow check?"

"Absolutely," said Aunt Terry. "I'll use the time to organize this box so we know what we have."

"You in?" Brent asked Josh.

ADVENTURE USA

"Sure," Josh said, sounding way braver than he felt. He could have used that report as an excuse. But banishing the loser image Brent had of him was way more important.

After lunch, the twins followed Brent down the path to the barn. They brought out the sled and helped lay the gangline in front of it.

Dark clouds had gathered in the distance. "If it were summer, I'd think a thunderstorm was coming," Josh said.

"The weather report predicted a chance of heavy snow tomorrow," said Brent. "But that system is far away. We've got time."

"Once a thunderstorm rolled in over the lake at home, and in minutes it hit land," said Lizzie. "It was pretty scary."

Brent hooked up Midnight. "We're not going far. Even if it snows, I know the way home."

He turned to Josh. "Do you want to finish hooking up Popsicle?"

"Okay," Josh started, his heart suddenly beating like a set of bongo drums. Brent held Popsicle with one hand and the tug line with the other. It would only take a second to snap it onto her harness.

Josh reached for the tug line. He felt his hand trembling inside his glove. *Come on*, he thought, ashamed of his fear. *You can do this!* Taking a deep breath, Josh snapped Popsicle onto the gangline.

"You're a pro!" Brent watched Popsicle wag her tail

Snapping to the Gangline

like an orchestra conductor. "She likes you."

Josh smiled. Slowly, almost without thinking, he reached out and gently petted Popsicle's head.

"Look at that!" Lizzie cried. "You're buddies!" She pumped her fist in the air. "I can taste that luscious chocolate peanut butter cup!"

Josh rolled his eyes. "I just gave her a little pat."

Lizzie rubbed her hands together, looking greedy. "But you're close. You're really close."

She moved beside Brent to film him snapping on the other dogs as Josh arranged a blanket in the sled.

"This will be the fifth post for my blog," Lizzie exclaimed, smiling. "The whole family has been leaving comments, including those Bradshaw cousins in Montana we rarely hear from."

"Nice," said Josh as he got into the sled. Lizzie positioned herself in front of him.

"Ready?" Brent asked.

Lizzie gave him a thumbs-up.

"Hike!" Brent cried.

The dogs took off down the trail like a shot from a cannon. Josh began to relax. Towering pine trees whizzed by them as they flew down the trail.

"Pretty cool, huh?" Lizzie said from the front.

"Very cool." Josh pulled the blanket up and thought about how much he was enjoying the sled. Not the *dogs*, just the sled.

Chapter 12
Apprentice Musher

The sled tore up a small hill into a clearing. Brent called, "*Whoa!*" and braked, bringing the dogs to a halt. "Welcome to Takuta Lake. It's filled from the Little Susitna River and eventually flows into the Gulf of Alaska."

Josh climbed out of the sled to look around.

"How can you tell the difference between an enormous field and a lake?" asked Lizzie from under the blanket.

"I know the area," said Brent. "There aren't many huge fields that run into this trail. Plus, I started a race here last year."

He pulled his hood over his helmet. "I lost control at the beginning. I got on an icy trail, and the claw brake wasn't sticking. I never made up the time."

Apprentice Musher

Josh scanned the edge of the lake through the binoculars.

"What are you searching for?" asked Brent.

"Steam," said Josh.

"I'm impressed."

Josh grinned.

"Like steam from a tea kettle?" Lizzie wanted to know. She had her phone ready to film it if they got close.

"A giant tea kettle," said Josh. "Experienced mushers look for steam coming up through the snow on a lake. It means there's a break in the ice."

"Last year an entire team—driver, dogs, and their sled—slid into a frozen whirlpool," Brent said. "Pulls you right in and—"

"A frozen whirlpool?" interrupted Lizzie. "How does that happen?"

"When it's super cold, all kinds of things freeze in Alaska," said Brent. "But there are rivers that flow all winter. Under the ice. If the ice isn't thick enough—"

"—down you go," finished Josh.

"Yikes!" Lizzie said.

"Fortunately, there was help nearby," added Brent.

"The dogs can warn you, though, right?" said Josh.

Brent nodded. "You've got to pay attention to them. Especially the lead dogs. If they act odd, something's up." He pointed to Midnight. "Their faces express fear, happiness, and worry, just like a human's. Watch their tails too."

ADVENTURE USA

Josh looked at Popsicle. Her tail was straight up and wagging. "What's Popsicle saying?"

"She says, 'Quit the talking. Let's go!'" Brent stepped off the runners. "How about another quick lesson? It's not icy today, so we won't have trouble stopping."

Lizzie snuggled deeper under the blanket. "Not for me. I'm staying right here."

Josh's heart started another drum roll. He'd love to tear down the trail on the sled, the dogs dashing ahead of him. Mushing the sled wasn't the same as being with the dogs, exactly. He'd have the sled in front of him for protection.

Josh's mouth was dry. "I guess—" he started. "I could give it a try."

"All right, Josh!" cried Lizzie, as she climbed out of the sled holding her phone. "I've got to get a video of this."

"Will the team respond to me?" Josh felt himself sweating in the frigid air.

"For sure," said Brent. "And I'll be right here. You won't have to worry about turns or giving the 'trail' command. That's when another musher calls '*Trail!*' in order to pass. That can be tricky," added Brent.

"What commands do I need?" asked Josh.

"There are just a few," said Brent. "*Hike* or *Let's go* is how I usually start them."

Brent showed Josh how to position himself on the runners.

Then he stood behind him.

"What about mush?" asked Lizzie.

"Mush is for the movies," said Brent. "Most people use *Hike*. We use *Whoa* to stop."

With a final clip of Josh ready to go, Lizzie stopped filming and climbed back into the sled.

"If you want to go left, you pull the handlebar slightly to the left and shout, *Haw*," Brent continued. "If you want to go right, you pull the handlebar a bit to the right and shout, *Gee*."

Josh clung to the handlebar. The brutal wind whipped around his body.

"Ready?" Brent asked.

Josh nodded.

"Then go ahead and take off," Brent said. "I'll lift the brake and be ready to step on it if we need to."

"*Hike!*" Josh shouted.

The huskies took off across the lake. The runners seemed to crackle as they skimmed over the surface.

Josh's face relaxed into a grin. He had never felt such freedom. He felt like he was flying.

"*Gee!*" Josh shouted to the team as he leaned the handlebar to the right. He watched as the huskies made the turn. They traveled along the edge of the lake, which led to a riverside trail.

Josh called, "*Haw!*" to bring them back around to the left. As they neared their starting point, Josh shouted, "*Whoa!*" while Brent braked. The team came to a stop on the far side of the lake.

"Just like a professional!" Brent exclaimed.

Josh beamed. "But that's because you were here."

Brent shook his head. "Most important is that the dogs believe they're in good hands. If they trust you, they'll listen to you."

"You make it look so easy."

"Like anything else, it's just practice." Brent knelt and rubbed Midnight and Thunder.

Lizzie had the binoculars out. "What are those sharp peaks in the distance?"

"Could be jumble ice. Sometimes a river freezes, thaws, separates, and refreezes. Ice peaks can form," Brent said. "It could rip the dogs and your sled to shreds. Last year it put one musher in the hospital with two broken legs. He was lucky. It could have been much worse."

Brent took off his backpack and pulled out a thermos. "Hot chocolate anyone?"

"Just what we need!" cried Lizzie.

The trio sat on a hill and enjoyed the delicious taste of the warm drink. Brent held up a small container. "Anyone for paniktak?"

"Pan-a what?" asked Lizzie.

Apprentice Musher

"*Paniktak*," repeated Brent. "A real Alaskan treat."

"Why not?" Josh put a piece in his mouth. It tasted fishy. "Not bad."

"I'll stick with something I know," Lizzie said, holding up the cocoa.

Brent laughed. "You'd be surprised at the things you've already eaten up here."

"What do you mean?" asked Lizzie. "Are you going to tell me we had moose or something like that?"

"Dad's stew last night? It was moose. The night before it was reindeer." Brent hooted at her surprised look.

"Why didn't you tell me?" Lizzie said.

"As for the paniktak," Brent went on, grinning, "it's dried meat. Like jerky. You've already had it."

"Breakfast?" Lizzie sputtered.

Brent nodded. "That casserole you had two helpings of."

"Gosh! This is nothing like New Jersey." Lizzie slouched into the snowbank. "I guess it was better not to know."

Josh held up the thermos. "Anyone for seconds?"

Lizzie shook her head, and Brent held up his hand. "I'm fine. Thanks."

Josh glanced at the sky. The black clouds that had seemed far away back home had edged closer. "Shouldn't we get going? That storm looks like it's moving closer."

ADVENTURE USA

"Wouldn't be a bad idea." Brent looked at his watch. "I guess we'll start for the cabin. Are you sure you don't want another lesson, Lizzie?"

"No, thanks. I'm happy getting photos and videos for my blog."

Josh and Lizzie climbed into the sled, and Brent got into position at the back.

"*Let's go!*" he called. The huskies jumped into action, dashing toward the trail ahead of them.

Josh settled into the sled and tried to relax. He was having trouble shaking a nagging fear that something wasn't right. *This is silly*, he told himself. Things were going well. He'd petted a dog, and he'd had his first mushing experience.

In his heart, he knew what was gnawing at him.

They were on their way to meet Hank.

And his dogs.

Josh leaned back and tried to enjoy the view. He was probably worried for no reason. After all, Brent was there. It wasn't like he was all alone with no one else but Hank.

CHAPTER 13
Injured

"Josh drew his hood tighter against his face. "The temperature's dropping. My nose feels like it's freezing off."

"I'm toasty." Lizzie wiggled her feet beneath the blanket. "All except for my feet."

Josh grinned. "That's why Brent put on those arctic bunny boots. They weigh over six pounds each."

"I wonder what's the coldest it's ever been?"

"Cold enough for spit to freeze," said Josh.

"In your mouth or out of it?" Lizzie wondered.

"I guess that depends on whether your mouth is open."

"Who'd keep their mouth open in this weather?"

"Someone who keeps asking questions," said Josh.

"Ha ha." Lizzie pulled the blanket up to her nose. "I'm keeping my mouth covered just in case."

The sled whizzed down the trail, cutting crisply through the snow. A few times, the trail curved sharply to the left or right, and Josh felt like he'd go flying over the edge of the sled.

"A little too fast for me," said Lizzie. "It reminds me of the Tilt-A-Whirl on the boardwalk back home."

Josh had a big smile on his face. "Or the Thunder Alps roller coaster. I love it!"

He picked up the binoculars. "Brown box straight ahead—that must be the cabin."

"Let me see."

He handed the binoculars to Lizzie. In the distance, he could barely make out a small shack.

"Almost there," Brent called from the back. He steered the sled over one last hill and slowed for the final curve.

As they came around the bend, Josh cried, "Look out!"

Up ahead, Hank lay sprawled in the snow. Blood dotted the ground near his legs. Lunging forward, Hank desperately tried to hold on to his sled as his team yipped and howled beneath a grove of pine trees.

Brent screamed, "*Whoa!*" as he brought his team to a stop on the other side of the trail and stomped on his snow hook.

"Grab my snow hook!" yelled Hank.

Injured

"I don't see it!" cried Brent.

"Here's the snub line!" Josh shouted. He scrambled to secure the rope around a nearby tree.

Meanwhile, Brent had found the snow hook. He jammed it into the ground before rushing to Hank's side. "What happened?"

Hank rolled over on his back and closed his eyes. Then he opened them and tried to sit up. "There was a moose on the path and—"

"Moose?" Brent interrupted. "Up here? Are you sure?"

Hank's eyes seemed to pierce the bitter cold. "Of course, I'm sure."

"We'll have to report it." Brent was thoughtful. "Let the Association know you sighted one so no one else will be surprised like you were."

Josh peered at the path.

"Tracks?" Lizzie whispered.

"Nothing," Josh mouthed.

"The team went crazy and jumped the path," Hank continued. "I felt myself falling, and I couldn't grab the snow hook."

"You're lucky you're not alone. You certainly don't want fresh blood on the trail up here." Brent bent over and looked at Hank's leg. "It almost looks like a bear mauled you. These tears look like teeth marks."

Hank scowled at Brent. "I think I can tell a bear from a moose."

Brent picked up the supplies that had fallen from Hank's sled. He held up a long black stick with a thin lash at the end. "What's up with this whip, Hank? You know the rules."

"It's for emergencies," Hank spat out, his words defiant.

Brent stared at Hank. "You're not whipping your team? You know that's forbidden."

Hank snickered. "What is this? The student instructs the teacher? I know the rules. As I said, just for emergencies. Wild animals and such."

Brent shook his head. "I'm not sure I'd even carry it. Someone who doesn't know you might get the wrong idea."

Hank's beady eyes met Brent's and then moved to Josh. "If someone *did* get the wrong idea, I'd have to figure out a way to change his mind."

Josh stayed where he was on the trail. He didn't want to get any closer to Hank than he had to.

He knew this much: moose had grinding and chewing teeth. Not tearing or ripping teeth.

Dogs had teeth like that. And they would use them to defend themselves.

Chapter 14

Marooned

Brent looked at Hank. "Where's your helmet?"

"Don't need one," said Hank. "They're not mandatory."

"True. But they could save your life. Come on," said Brent. "Let's get you in the cabin. I've got a first aid kit. We can clean up your wounds and get you home. Are you strong enough to stand?"

"Of course, I can stand." Hank took hold of a thick branch. Using it as a crutch, he forced himself to his feet. "It's only a minor scrape."

But as soon as Hank put weight on his leg, he collapsed. "Guess I'm a little dizzy, that's all."

Brent motioned for Josh. "Get on the other side of him. We'll guide him inside."

Josh moved to Hank's right, but Hank brushed him off angrily. "I said I'm fine. Get out of my way."

Josh stepped back as Hank hobbled a few feet to the cabin. Lizzie got there ahead of him and held open the door.

Brent watched as the two disappeared inside. "He's got a mind of his own, doesn't he?"

Josh nodded and tried to swallow the lump in his throat.

Brent put his hand on Josh's shoulder. "Don't worry. Hank's all talk. Deep down he respects the rules."

Yeah, right, thought Josh. His opinion of Hank certainly hadn't improved in the last few minutes. If anything, his worry had doubled.

Rechecking that the teams and sleds were securely anchored, Josh and Brent went to the cabin. They found Hank lying on a tattered rug in the center of the room. One leg of his snow pants was unzipped, and Lizzie held a cloth to his wound.

Brent opened his pack and took out his first aid kit. "We'll clean and bandage it, and you'll be as good as new—"

"He's got a nasty gash." Lizzie moved the blood-soaked cloth so they could see.

Brent bent down to look. "Are you sure there wasn't a coyote or wolf along with that moose? These are teeth marks; I'm sure of it. You might want to get a rabies shot to be sure."

Hank closed his eyes and then opened them. "I told you, I got pulled over rough terrain. I felt the branches ripping my leg as I was dragged."

Marooned

Josh grabbed a new piece of gauze and covered the wound. Immediately, the blood soaked through. "That gash is deep, and the femoral artery runs down the lower leg."

Hank pushed himself up on his elbows, a smirk on his face. "Well, Little Nurse. Isn't it nice that Brent brought you along? In case we need some medical advice."

Stung by Hank's words, Josh looked at Brent and shrugged. "I read a lot. Last summer I was really into biology. Anyway," Josh continued, "we need to stop the bleeding. That's urgent. A person can go into shock easily from the loss of blood."

Hank pushed himself up further, then collapsed on the floor. "Stop being so dramatic! Wipe it down, throw a bandage on it, and we're off. I've had worse wounds from mosquito bites."

Brent stood up and stared at Hank. "I'm afraid you're not going anywhere in this treacherous weather." He held up his hand when Hank started to protest. "Here's the plan. Your sled is smaller, so I'll mush your team back with Lizzie and get help. Josh can stay with you."

Brent was still talking, but Josh didn't hear a word he was saying. His mind was whirling with the thought of being marooned in this isolated cabin with Hank.

An injured and angry Hank.

"Come on, Lizzie. Let's go," said Brent.

Lizzie stood up. "Maybe I should stay with Josh and help."

"No point in risking three people's lives in this cold,"

Brent said. "Josh has a handle on what to do if the bleeding starts up again."

Zipping up his coat, Brent headed for the door. Josh was right behind him. "What about us all going back together?" he asked, desperation in his voice.

"Hank shouldn't be bouncing around in a sled," said Brent. "Look, you've got this. Keep him comfortable. I'll be back in an hour at the most."

Lizzie's eyes met Josh's. "Are you going to be all right?" she whispered.

"Come... right... back!" Josh mouthed fiercely.

Outside, Brent positioned himself on Hank's sled, pulled up the snow hook, and called over his shoulder, "You probably know more about first aid than I do. You're the man, Josh."

No, I'm not, thought Josh.

Brent held up his hand in a wave. "You'll be fine."

"You're wrong," whispered Josh. "Maybe even dead wrong."

Chapter 15

A Dangerous Plan

Josh trudged into the cabin and closed the door tightly behind him. It was only slightly warmer inside than outside. But at least the wind wasn't whipping around them.

Across the room, Hank leaned over on his side and glared. "If you think I'm going to sit here and wait for someone to come back and get me, you're nuts!"

Gripped with fear, Josh approached Hank. Blood had oozed over the sides of the bandage and was trickling down his leg.

"The bleeding has to be stopped," Josh said. He pulled more gauze and a wide roll of elastic bandage from the first aid kit.

Carefully, he replaced the gauze, pressing it against Hank's leg. "I'll apply steady pressure to the wound. Then we'll wrap it and elevate it."

"You can play nurse all you want." Hank swatted Josh's hands away. "But not on me. I'm getting out of here." He pressed the gauze in place while he wrapped some tape around his leg. Then with a series of grunts and the help of his branch crutch, he managed to get to his feet.

"I didn't come all this way to sit in some remote shack," Hank growled. "I came to explore the North Trail. And some kid playing nurse won't stop me."

"You're injured and losing blood! You could collapse on the trail!"

"Shut your mouth." Hank's face wore a furious sneer. "You can stay here and freeze." He hobbled to the door on his crutch. "Try to stop me!"

Josh rushed toward him. "Hank, please wait. Brent will be back soon! It's much too far to walk—"

Hank whirled around, the door half open and snow billowing in from outside. "Walk? What are you talking about?"

"The trail. You can't walk off by yourself!" Josh cried. "You could collapse."

"I'm not walking anywhere. There's a team of brutes out there who can take me wherever I want to go."

A Dangerous Plan

Hank seized the whip he had left by the door. "They say a storm is coming. Perfect conditions for a training run."

Josh panicked. Hank with a whip! Hank with the team! "That's Brent's team. You can't—" Josh sputtered.

Hank stretched out the crutch, so it was under Josh's chin. "That's where you're wrong, Little Nurse. I can. And I will."

Josh was horrified. This couldn't be happening. Whipping was cruel and could ruin the team. It could make them scared and turn on each other, not to mention the driver. It would take Brent months to get them back into shape. Months he didn't have before the county finals.

"But they may not respond to—" Josh started.

"Oh, they'll mind me, all right." Hank pulled his hat lower on his forehead. "It won't take them long to figure out who's the boss around here."

Josh lunged desperately for the whip. Enraged, Hank twirled around on the crutch. The whip snapped in the air, and its tip stung Josh's wrist like a sizzling brand. He rubbed his wrist, a welt already beginning to form.

"I'm not going to have trouble with you now, am I?" Hank snarled. "Get in the sled and keep your mouth shut. I'd leave you here, but I might need your help later."

Josh's mouth was dry. His heart pounded. What should he do? He knew he only had one choice. He couldn't leave the dogs in the hands of this madman. He'd have to go along and hope

ADVENTURE USA

Hank was in better shape than he thought. Hope they'd beat the storm. Hope they'd make it back home.

Alive.

CHAPTER 16

Trouble on the Trail

Outside, the dogs were howling. Josh knew they sensed something was wrong.

"I said, get in the sled!" Hank growled.

Josh held his ground. "Please don't use the whip on this team. Maybe your dogs are used to it, but—"

Up ahead, Nova barked sharply, showing his teeth.

Hank grimaced and sucked in his breath. "Quit yakking and get in! Dogs do better with a master. Soon they'll know who's in charge!"

Josh was terrified, but he knew what he had to do. Inching toward the dogs, he called out softly at first and then louder. "It's all right, Nova. That's a girl, Midnight. Good job, Thunder."

"I said, GET IN!" Hank cracked the whip over his head. "You waste any more time, and I'll use this on you!"

Josh was far enough away that he knew Hank couldn't reach him. He made his way through the rest of the dogs, resting his hand lightly on them for reassurance. He felt he should do more, but every time he touched the dogs, he was petrified. Still, he felt a familiar presence might be enough to calm them down.

"NOW!" Hank screamed into the bone-chilling air. "This is your last warning!"

Josh faced Hank. "You won't use that on me. And you won't use that on the dogs."

Hank's lip curled into an ugly sneer. "I only use what's necessary. Now get in or stay here and freeze."

Josh thought about wrestling the whip from him but rejected the idea. Hank was injured and Josh was fast, but Hank's massive arms and hands were still capable of harm. Josh would do the best he could to protect himself and the dogs.

Reluctantly, he climbed into the sled, knowing how limited his options were. When he turned his head, he saw Hank had one hand on the handlebar and the other on his crutch. The whip was stuck in the belt, which encircled the waist of his parka. His face was contorted in pain.

No sooner had Josh positioned himself safely in the sled than the team tore down the trail. He knew Hank was in no condition to be cautious, so Josh watched for signs of danger.

Trouble on the Trail

Up ahead, the path seemed clear. But he knew his instincts were probably the only thing standing between them and disaster.

Josh hoped they'd meet up with another racer. There might be others checking out the trail like they were—someone, anyone, who could help.

As they sprinted through a forested path and into a wide-open field, Josh scanned the trail. Suddenly, in the distance, he saw jagged white peaks. His eyes wide with terror, he immediately recognized the danger.

"Watch out!" Josh cried.

"What is it now?" Hank growled.

"Jumble ice ahead!" Josh shrieked. He started to sweat again as he took stock of the trail. It was dotted with spears of ice.

Whipping around, he tried to get Hank's attention again. "Slow down!" he screamed.

"Ha!" Hank snarled. "The expert speaks again. Dogs can handle it."

Hank fingered the whip jammed in his belt. "If not, I have ways of convincing them."

Then without warning, the path jerked to the left, where a narrow trail bordered the ice. Midnight and Thunder, used to taking curves as a team, easily accommodated for the twist. The swing dogs, Popsicle and Boots, had only a little less success. But Vortex and Nova swung too far, causing the sled to slam against a tree.

Hank, shaky and barely managing to hold on, was tossed off the back like a bag of garbage.

Josh barely had time to shout out a desperate, "*Whoa!*" before he, too, was dumped from the sled. Helpless to stop himself, he careened over the ice and snow headfirst.

CHAPTER 17

Disaster

When he opened his eyes, all Josh could see was white. He tried to move, but the pain in his ankle stopped him. Dazed, he wondered if he'd be able to stand. He reached for his head and felt his helmet. It had probably saved his life.

He stared up at the trees. The bare branches reminded him of thin fingers drawing on the sky. Suddenly, he was aware of a low moaning. He tried again to rise but slumped back to the ground.

The sled was nearby. Miraculously, it was still in one piece. Tipped over on its side, it was wedged between two large trees. The dogs stood in a twisted mass. They yipped into the bitter cold air, waiting for a command.

ADVENTURE USA

Josh rolled over. With the help of a low branch, he got to his knees. He didn't feel like anything was broken, but maybe a sprain was causing the pain. Mustering all his remaining strength, he pulled himself up the rest of the way. His legs trembled as he put weight on them. He clutched onto the branch for support.

"Hank!" Josh cried into the stillness. "Hank!"

The only answer was the wind whistling through the trees.

Josh tried screaming louder. "HANK!"

Up ahead, inches from a tree, the dogs huddled in a pack. Nova turned and snarled.

Josh had a dreadful thought. *Did the dogs think this was his fault? What if they turned on him?*

"It's all right, Nova. Good girl, Midnight," he called to the team.

Frantically, Josh enlarged his search. He staggered behind each tree, each mound. Nothing.

As a last resort, he forced himself over a nearby ridge. There, in a small field, was Hank. Blood oozed from a wound on his face. His eyes were closed.

Josh dropped to his knees and crawled to him.

"Hank!" Josh cried.

No answer.

Josh reached out and turned Hank's head to face him. "Hank! It's Josh!"

Hank lay silent on the snow-covered ground.

Disaster

Josh tried again. "Hank! Wake up!"

Hank's eyes half opened, then closed, then fluttered open. He tried to push himself up. "Get..." he uttered before collapsing.

"Hank!" Josh cried. He felt for Hank's pulse and found it. But it seemed faint.

Hank's mouth hung open, but no more sounds came out.

Josh trembled as he stared at the man.

What could they do now? Brent would never find them in this frozen wasteland. Josh cringed when he thought about all the things he should have done. Beginning with the note that he should have left in the cabin. He took out his cell phone. No bars. No service.

Josh stared through the trees at the dogs.

The dogs.

Suddenly, the horrifying truth hit him like an avalanche.

His life. The dogs.

Hank.

They were all in his hands now.

Chapter 18

It's Up to Josh

F illed with anguish, Josh closed his eyes. He felt like throwing up. Easing himself to his knees and then to his feet, he hobbled across the snow toward the sled. He pulled the blanket loose and rummaged in the sled basket.

Had Brent put in the survival backpack? Josh hadn't seen him bring it out.

Josh reached deep into the toe of the sled. There it was! He yanked it out and located the emergency space blankets, then slowly limped toward Hank. Shaking out the blankets, he carefully tucked them around Hank's body.

Hank was motionless.

Josh knew he had to work fast. His heart hammering,

It's Up to Josh

he dragged himself back to the sled. He pulled on the handlebar, but the sled was wedged tight between the trees. The more he tugged, the more it held.

With a sense of dread, Josh realized he'd have to unsnap the gangline from the sled to free it. But first, he would have to use the snow hook to secure the dogs.

Unsnap the gangline? Secure the dogs? Was he kidding? How could he possibly do that?

Tears welled up in his eyes, and his lips trembled uncontrollably. Josh took a deep breath, refusing to sink further into despair.

No good feeling sorry for myself, he thought. His ankle throbbing, he began a slow crawl around the sled to Popsicle.

Josh's knees bumped against the icy ridges of the crusty snow. He stopped a foot in front of Popsicle. What was she thinking? Did she know how terrified he was?

Popsicle barked. Several of the other dogs did the same. Then the team exploded with shrieking howls.

His heart beating in his throat, Josh inched his hand out to her. She nudged his glove with her black nose. Gently, he touched the top of her head.

"You've got to help me, girl," he whispered. "We've got to get back home."

Trembling, Josh grabbed a low-hanging branch and pulled himself closer to the sled. Josh wasn't sure how to start, so he began by detaching the gangline from the sled so he could move it. In seconds, he panicked and realized the mistake he had made. He had forgotten to secure the team before he detached the gangline! Now there was nothing to hold back the dogs.

Desperately, Josh tried to resnap the gangline. The dogs hadn't bolted, but they moved restlessly, and the line tightened. His hands felt clumsy in his thick gloves. He opened the hook and thrust it toward the loop, pulling with all his strength. Each time, he missed the loop. He gripped the hook again as tight as he could. He edged it forward, still pinching it. Just as it snapped into place, the team surged forward. Josh knew he would have been yanked behind them like a rag doll. Fortunately, the sled was wedged between the trees and held the team back.

He grabbed the snow hook and jammed it into the icy ground. Immediately, it toppled over. Desperate, he searched for a crevice and tried again. This time it seemed to hold. Rising to his feet, he stomped on it several times with his boot. He bent over to test it. It was solid!

With a jolt, Josh realized the tug lines were twisted. Brent had said the dogs could be injured if the tugs were too tight. Somehow, Josh would have to unsnap the dogs from their neck and tug lines, untwist the tugs, and resnap the hooks.

Sweat trickling down his back, Josh started with Midnight. Carefully, he unsnapped her from the gangline, untwisted the line, and resnapped her in. As he did, he brushed snowflakes off

It's Up to Josh

his face. He hadn't noticed the dark clouds overtake the gray sky. Tiny flakes were flying furiously now.

Josh doubled his speed, trying to stay calm as he unsnapped each dog's hook and straightened the lines. Finally, it was Popsicle's turn. Josh unsnapped her hook and was turning over the tug line when what looked like a fox shot through the underbrush. With a flash, Popsicle tore after it, ripping the tug line from his hand.

"Popsicle!" Josh cried. "Popsicle, come back!"

He scanned the snowy landscape for any sign of movement. Nothing!

NO! He couldn't have lost a dog! What would he do now? How would they get back without a full team? Josh collapsed on the ground in frustration.

Tears stung his eyes as he rolled over and stared at the sky. What was he doing out here in the wilderness with dogs and a sled? A sob choked out as he turned over.

Trying to get home alive.

Josh pushed himself up. He had to keep working. He couldn't stop for one dog. He had to get Hank loaded in the sled and back home before darkness and the blizzard set in. Now was their only chance.

Josh moved through the team again, hoping the snow hook would hold the dogs. Seizing the gangline, he disconnected it from the sled. Then he clasped the handlebar and pulled on the sled to dislodge it. It wouldn't budge.

ADVENTURE USA

Finally, he braced himself against a nearby tree, dug his boots into a ridge for leverage, and pulled with all his might. Suddenly, with a *crack*, the sled came free, knocking him over. Exhausted, he crawled to where it had stopped. As he pushed it onto its runners, he saw the left runner had a fine crack on one side. He hoped they could get home without it breaking.

His ankle aching with sharp jabs of pain, he pushed the sled toward Hank. Josh slid the blankets away from him and spread them out on the snow. Hank moaned softly.

"I'm going to try to roll you onto this blanket." He wasn't sure if Hank heard him but talking helped keep Josh calm. "We'll take it slow." He realized a bone could be broken and by moving Hank, he could make it worse. But he also knew he had no other choice. If they didn't get back to the farm, they'd both die out there.

Josh tucked a blanket up against Hank and carefully rolled him onto it, remembering that first aid course at school. Next, he used a piece of rope from the survival bag to tie the top and bottom corners of the blanket together. This made a sturdy sling that would prevent Hank from slipping out.

Pulling fiercely on one end of the blanket, Josh slid Hank toward the sled. The going was slow as the wind whipped around them, and Josh moved with great care so as not to increase Hank's injuries. If only Hank were able to help! But soft moans were all that came from the blanket.

It's Up to Josh

At last, with a final burst of energy, Josh slid Hank over the lip of the sled and positioned him as comfortably as possible. Grabbing the other blanket, he tucked it around Hank to protect his face.

By now the wind had picked up. Josh pulled his hood back over his helmet, and exhausted, he collapsed to his knees. He closed his eyes, but only for a moment this time. Across the snow were the dogs. He could do this; he had to.

Slowly, Josh stood up. He adjusted his neck gaiter and drew his hood tighter. He had to attach the gangline, something he'd only watched Brent do once. But he knew this much: he had to be strong. Animals could smell fear even better than people.

Determined, he went forward to the dogs. They barked and pranced around him, eager to run. He checked the snow hook. It was still holding. He hoped the team wouldn't take off once he released it. What would he do then?

Suddenly, he knew. The snub line could hold them. Grabbing it, Josh wrapped it twice around a nearby tree and tied a quick-release knot.

Josh took a deep breath and crept between the dogs, trying to reassure and encourage them. "Good boy!" he said, his voice squeaky with fear.

"Good girl!" He spoke louder this time, trying to sound confident as if this were part of a regular day.

Josh felt awkward in his thick gloves, but he knew he couldn't risk taking them off. Carefully, he reattached the gangline to the sled. He checked to be sure the tug line for each dog was secure.

Finally, it was time. Josh moved to the back of the sled. As he got on, he heard a noise. A gentle pounding that seemed to get louder. Josh jerked his head to the right. The sound was coming closer.

Please, thought Josh, *not more trouble.*

Josh whirled around to see a furry white ball rush up and nuzzle his legs.

Popsicle! She was back!

He slowly knelt and hugged her, forgetting his fears. Was he ever glad to see Popsicle!

Josh hooked her to the gangline and connected her neckline. Then he got back on the sled. With a last glance around the darkening forest, he yanked on the snow hook to release it and pulled on the quick-release knot to untie the snub line.

Taking a deep, quivering breath, Josh gripped the handlebar. "*Hike!*" he cried.

With a powerful leap forward, the team took off down the narrow path.

Chapter 19

Snowmobile

The dogs quickly got into their pace as the sled shot down the trail. Josh had to keep ducking to avoid the overhanging branches. Nervously, he slid his hands along the top of the handlebar. The speed was a little too fast for him, and he considered trying to slow down. Once he had seen Brent drag his foot to decrease the speed. Josh tried it but nearly fell off. *Better keep my feet on the runners*, he thought. He couldn't risk losing his balance.

Josh pulled his hood tighter around his face. Even though the air had to be well below freezing, he still felt sweaty from the stress. He kept his eyes on the trail, watching for trouble as they sped through the forest. He couldn't stop to check on Hank, but he hoped he was all right.

The team ran expertly along the trail. Every group of trees they sped past brought them closer to home.

Dashing out of the forest into an open field, the team approached Takuta Lake. Suddenly, in the distance, Josh spied steam coming off the lake. The team was aiming right for it.

"*Gee!*" Josh called, hoping there was a trail along the side.

There was! Thunder and Midnight easily found it, and Josh breathed a brief sigh of relief as the trail wound away from the lake.

Josh glimpsed the light dimming on the horizon. The red and purple of the sunset were breathtaking but a reminder that night was coming fast. He had to make it home before dark, or they'd be stuck in the woods for the night.

Up ahead, they approached another cluster of trees. Traveling through the forest paths, Josh felt even more afraid. It was much darker. Was there a headlamp in the survival backpack? If only he had thought to check.

As they entered the path, the team picked up more speed. The first curve was way too sharp. *We need to slow down*, thought Josh. But there was no mushing command for that.

Josh thrust down the brake. The team slowed, and he sighed with relief.

The forest was silent except for the skimming of the sled and the sound of the dogs panting. Then, in the distance, there was a new sound. Josh pushed back his hood and heard a low hum. The sound was familiar, yet he couldn't identify it.

Snowmobile

Suddenly, the noise became louder—a clattering, growling sound. An instant later, he knew. Snowmobilers! Trees surrounded him on both sides. There was no room for him to veer to either side.

The motors grew louder and louder. In minutes the snowmobilers would come crashing down the trail. Up ahead, he could barely see a tiny clearing on the left. In desperation, Josh frantically screamed, "*Haw! Haw!*"

Would the dogs listen? The roar of the snowmobilers was right behind him. Josh dragged the brake as he screamed again, "*Haw!*"

Just in time, Midnight and Thunder pulled the team over. The sled teetered as it careened into the small clearing.

"*Whoa!*" Josh cried as he pressed harder on the brake. He felt the rush of wind slap his face as the snowmobilers streaked past.

"Help! Help!" he screamed to them, but they vanished into the night.

Josh gripped the handlebar and took a breath. He tried to determine if the team was tangled, but it was hard to see in the forest. They seemed to be fine. He hoped he was right.

Josh checked on Hank. His eyes were shut. "Hank? Hank, please stay awake!"

Hank's eyes fluttered and then closed. Josh hoped he wasn't in shock.

"Open your eyes!" he pleaded. "We're almost home."

ADVENTURE USA

Exhausted, Josh let out a sigh. He didn't have any idea how far away they were.

Quickly, he took off the backpack and unzipped it. Plunging his hand inside, he soon felt the rectangular shape of the headlamp. He pulled it over his helmet and secured it. After he flicked it on, light flooded the path. He could see so much better!

He clutched the handlebar and steadied himself on the runners before releasing the brake. When he screamed, *"Hike!"* into the twilight, he barely recognized his voice; it sounded so much stronger.

The team tore down the narrow forest path. With all the twists and turns, Josh found once again that he needed to shift his weight from one foot to the other to stay balanced. Suddenly, he remembered that cracked runner. *Please make it hold*, he thought.

Now the team was making good time. Josh ducked to avoid being slapped in the face by another fir branch. There was nothing but towering pine trees bordering the trail. He hoped the dogs knew the way. It all looked the same to him. What if they met a fork in the trail? Would they know what to do? Would he?

Ba-dum, ba-dum, ba-dum. The dogs' pounding paws created a mesmerizing rhythm.

Josh felt his concentration slipping. He was beyond exhausted. With all the strength he could muster, he fought to stay focused.

Snowmobile

A little longer. Just a little longer, he thought. His fingers, with their death grip on the handlebar, went into a painful cramp. Josh opened and closed his left hand and did the same with his right. Then he hung on with everything he had as the team bolted through the snow.

Up ahead, Josh thought he could see a patch of pure white. Could it be the field just beyond Brent's house? As the team dashed down the path toward an even larger circle of white, Josh was almost certain they were approaching the farm.

Finally, the team burst out of the forest into a large clearing. There in the distance was the sweetest sight he had ever seen. A lone silo rose from the field. He could barely discern a tiny red flag fluttering from the top.

They were nearly there. They had done it!

Josh murmured a prayer of thanks. "Popsicle! Do you see what I see?"

Chapter 20
Across the Field

"*Whoa!*" Josh cried as the team raced across the field toward the house. He could see flashlights waving in the night.

"*Whoa!*" Josh called again to the team as he put pressure on the brake. Several people rushed toward him through the whirling lights of the police cars.

The dogs slowed to a stop near the dog yard. Trembling, Josh limped off the runners.

Emergency medical technicians rushed to the sled.

"Josh!" Lizzie tore across the yard with a blanket. When she reached him, she wrapped it around his shoulders in a bear hug. "You're safe!"

Across the Field

"Hhe wwouldn't lllllisten—" Josh's teeth chattered as he spoke.

Brent was right behind Lizzie. "We went back to the cabin and found it empty. We were just organizing a second search party for you. You're the *man*, Josh."

Despite the cold, Josh felt warmth spread through his body. He broke into a smile. *Maybe I am*, he thought.

Aunt Terry's mouth dropped open when she saw him. "We figured you had trouble. But we didn't know how much trouble." She wrapped another blanket around him. "Come right inside. There's plenty of time to talk later. The EMTs will want to check you."

Still shivering, Josh clung to the blankets like they were a life preserver. "Hank wouldn't listen. He wanted to take the dogs up the North Trail."

"You're a brave boy," Officer Nelson said.

Josh nodded. The lump in his throat made talking almost impossible.

"They say a blizzard's coming," said Officer Nelson, gesturing to the snow that had already covered the windshields. "Not a good day for an accident."

"Hank said he hit a moose," Josh started.

Officer Nelson's eyes got wide. "Moose up there near Takuta Lake? Never heard of that."

Josh turned to see some of the rescue team heading his

way. He knew he had to ask, even though his heart wasn't in it. "How's Hank?"

"Just came to. May have been in shock. Might have a concussion. They'll take him to the hospital," an EMT said. "I'd say you got here in the nick of time."

"He has a serious bite on his leg. Dog, probably," a woman in a thick orange vest said. "Any of his dogs sick?"

"He was wearing a whip," added the EMT. "They might have turned on him."

"Whips are forbidden," said Officer Nelson. "The Association is very strict about that."

"That explains the bites," the woman said. "Some people think you can beat your dogs into winning."

Relief washed over Josh, his suspicions confirmed. Across the path, his eyes met Brent's.

"Some mushers forget that dogs want to win," the EMT continued. "They're working with us, not against us."

Brent rubbed Popsicle's head. Then he said, "You were right, Josh."

Josh nodded as they continued congratulating the team.

When he had seen to all the dogs, Brent said, "You did an awesome job, Josh. The dogs knew they were safe with you. That's why they listened."

"What about Hank's dogs?" Josh asked. "Who will keep them safe?"

Across the Field

"I don't know," said Brent. "There'll be an investigation, for sure." He put his arm on Josh's shoulder. "How about some soup and paniktak?"

Josh smiled gratefully.

CHAPTER 21
Winner's Circle

"Hey!" called Josh as he galloped down the steps. "Save some pancakes for me!"

His dad helped himself to another. "There's more than enough for everyone," he said. "These are delicious, Terry. Wish we'd finished our research earlier."

"We had to hang around longer to speak to that naturalist who leads backcountry hikes," explained Mom. "But it was well worth it. They go into the glaciers, very appealing to many people."

"Your timing is perfect," said Uncle Bob.

"We get to go to the county finals together," cried Lizzie. "And at least it's a little warmer."

Winner's Circle

"Ha! Now it's twenty-two degrees instead of eighteen degrees!" said Josh.

"I guess you two have had enough of all this snow," said Mom. "Time to head home soon."

"But first the big race," added Josh, surprising himself with how different he felt from when they'd arrived.

After breakfast, the family got suited up in their winter parkas. Josh and Lizzie raced each other to the van.

"First!" yelled Josh.

"I don't like when I hear that," said Lizzie.

Dad followed the winding road through town. Their cousin's truck with the dog box was straight ahead. It had snowed again the previous night. A fresh blanket of white glistened in the morning light.

Their father pulled into the parking lot, and the twins jumped out. The noise was deafening with all the mushers and their teams. Brent was busy lifting the sled down.

"How do you feel this morning, Brent?" Mom wanted to know.

"Like I can win this race," he said. "I'm ready to go. My dogs are too."

Lizzie and Josh stood by the sled while Brent went to check in. He came back later with his number tied to his chest.

Once the dogs were harnessed, Brent approached the starting line. He made a last check of the lines and his sled.

ADVENTURE USA

A crowd of racers lined up ahead of him. He waved at Atasak and Will.

"Hey, Brent," called Will.

"Hey," said Brent.

"Ready to win?" Atasak said.

"I'm hoping to." Brent smiled. "And you?"

Atasak rubbed one of her dogs. "We're ready too."

The county finals also had a timed start. Brent found his name on the board to see what position he was in. Will was in the middle of the list, and Atasak's name was almost at the end.

Lizzie and Josh watched from behind the orange plastic fencing on each side of the route. As a racer got into position, an official steadied the front of the sled, holding it back from being pulled until the racer started.

A few racers moved into position and took off. Soon Brent was up. Lizzie pulled out the stopwatch and got ready to start it.

"On your mark!" cried the starting official. "Get ready! Five, four, three, two, one, GO!"

Lizzie set the stopwatch, and they cheered as Brent and his dogs dashed forward. The team tore down the trail.

Josh followed them with the binoculars. "They look good!"

"Go, Brent!" cried Lizzie.

In seconds, the team was almost out of sight.

"We've got some time," said Dad. "And I've got some hot chocolate. Let's go inside."

Winner's Circle

"Awesome," said Lizzie.

Inside the rustic clubhouse, family and friends of the racers milled around. Some huddled by the fireplace warming up while others stood talking in small groups.

Josh and Lizzie chose a seat on a bench nearby.

Lizzie let out a long breath. "Knock, knock."

"Who's there?" asked Josh.

"Ice."

"Ice who?"

"Ice a-hoping we'll be out of this cold soon," said Lizzie.

"Ice a-hoping the same thing," said Josh.

Mom handed steaming cups to Lizzie and Josh.

Josh took a sip. "Why does hot chocolate always taste so good?"

Dad smiled. "It tastes especially good today because it's so cold. Why, if we were in Hawaii—"

The twins' eyes got wide. "Are you trying to tell us something?" asked Josh.

Their father shrugged. "We haven't decided where we'll go next."

"But Hawaii is a possibility?" Lizzie said.

"Well, it's one of the fifty states," said Mom.

"Come on!" said Josh. "I want to know what's next."

Dad looked at the clock. "What's next is congratulating Brent at the finish line."

ADVENTURE USA

Josh rolled his eyes, and the twins savored the hot chocolate and cookies while they warmed up by the fire.

Soon they put their parkas back on and hurried out the door. As they crossed the parking lot to the field on the other side, they saw a lone figure with a shovel and a bucket. A young man was cleaning up the dog yard near the starting line.

"This time I'm positive who that is," whispered Lizzie. "It's Hank."

Josh watched as Hank slowly made his way around the enclosure.

Their aunt and uncle caught up with them. They noticed the twins staring at Hank.

"He had a concussion, a lot of bruising, numerous sprains, but no broken bones," said Uncle Bob. "Once he healed, they assigned him to community service for the rest of the season."

"He's got months of Saturday cleanup," Aunt Terry said.

"Plenty of time to think," added Uncle Bob.

The Parker family made their way over to the finish line. Many others had lined up behind the fencing, cheering for their friends.

Suddenly, in the distance, Josh spotted Brent's red parka.

"There he is!" He turned to Lizzie. "What kind of time is he making?"

"Thirty-seven minutes, forty seconds." Lizzie had her phone ready to capture Brent tearing over the finish line.

Winner's Circle

Brent and his team thundered closer. Josh fixed his eyes on the finish line. A gust of air swept over his face as Brent and his team burst through.

"Forty minutes, forty-three seconds!" cried the timing official.

A huge smile exploded on Brent's face. After securing the sled, he moved through his dog team, praising them one by one.

Lizzie and Josh jumped up and down screaming.

Brent tried to hug everyone in his family at the same time.

"I'm close!" he cried. "I finally broke forty-one minutes!"

"Is it fast enough to win?" Josh asked.

"I don't know," said Brent. "A lot of mushers are still on the course. Once all the racers finish, they'll compile the times. But we'll have to wait for the ceremony to see who the winners are."

Later, they gathered in the clubhouse, where officials were on stage preparing for the awards. The room was quickly filling up.

The Parker family found seats as close to the front as possible.

Josh, Lizzie, and Brent took off their hats and unzipped their parkas. "Whew, I'm warm," said Lizzie.

"Knock, knock," said Josh.

"Who's there?"

"Ina."

"Ina who?"

"Ina minute we'll find out who won." Josh laughed.

A woman approached the microphone. "We now have the results of the county finals." She held up a piece of paper and began to read. "Third place goes to Will Meetik of Palmer with a time of forty-one minutes, fifty-one seconds."

Applause filled the room as Will came forward for his trophy.

"Second place is Brent Parker of Hawk River with a time of forty minutes, forty-three seconds."

The Parker family jumped out of their seats, enveloping Brent in a group hug. Brent beamed as he rushed toward the stage to receive his trophy.

"Now for the first-place award and a cash prize of $5,000..." The announcer paused.

The crowd was silent with expectation.

"The winner is Atasak Palluq of Matanuska with a time of forty minutes, thirty seconds, a new trail record."

Atasak stood, and her family stood with her. Tears rolled down Atasak's face. Each family member laid a hand on her in praise as she passed them. At the end of the row, her father sat smiling in a wheelchair. Atasak bent to hug him, her shoulders shuddering.

Slowly, she mounted the steps and turned toward the audience. "Thank you so much!"

Winner's Circle

A race official brought out a giant cardboard check made out to Atasak. The two of them held it up as photographers snapped away.

Then Brent moved to the front. He put out his hand to congratulate Atasak. "I'm very happy for you, Atasak."

"The money will help so much." Atasak wiped her eyes with her sleeve. "It will give my father the time he needs to heal."

Brent returned to his seat and rejoined his family.

Uncle Bob put his arm around his son. "You're growing into quite a man, Brent."

"Thanks," Brent said. "I'm glad Atasak won. She needs the money right now. Much more than I do." He shrugged and then winked at his dad. "Besides, next month is the Knik Sprint with an even bigger prize pot."

Later, back at Parkerview Farm, Brent unloaded the team into the dog yard.

"Aren't you a little disappointed?" Lizzie wanted to know. "You worked so hard."

"Oh, sure," said Brent. "But I'm happy for Atasak. Besides, second place is also great!" He looked at his cousins. "How should we celebrate? Honey balls, anybody?"

"What?" cried Josh.

Brent chuckled. "How about honey balls for the team and cheese steaks for us?"

Josh knelt to hug Popsicle. "How about cheese steaks, French fries, and shakes?"

"Hey, who's the winner here?" Lizzie asked.

Josh took off his thick gloves. He barely noticed the scar on his wrist as he ran his fingers through Popsicle's thick fur. "I think we're all winners."

"You better believe it," whispered Lizzie. "You're a dog *lover*! I win!" She held out her hand. "My peanut butter cup, please."

"I guess that's one bet I don't mind paying," Josh said as Popsicle licked his face.

Please review...

Did you enjoy reading
ALASKA! Danger on the Mushing Trail?

Please consider taking a few minutes to write a review on Amazon or Goodreads. A review is very helpful in spreading the word to other readers. Thank you very much for your help.

Please join my ADVENTURE USA list of readers and be the first in your town to read my next book. Visit my website at https://barbaralarmonfailing.com and add your name to my list of readers.

I love hearing from children, parents, teachers (I previously taught first and fifth grades), librarians, booksellers, and anyone else who loves books.
I am available for in-person or Zoom visits.
Please get in touch at https://barbaralarmonfailing.com

I look forward to hearing from you!

Glossary

Booties — A type of sock that is made to protect a dog's feet from small cuts and sores. Various materials such as denim and polar fleece are used.

Bridle — A polyester rope that is attached to the stanchions on both sides of the sled. It is brought to the front where the gangline is attached to it.

Brush bow — (Rhymes with cow) An arched piece of heavy plastic or wood that is placed at the front of the sled. If there is a collision with a tree, snowbank, or other sled, it acts like a bumper, protecting the sled from damage.

Dropped dog — A dog that the musher has dropped from his team at a checkpoint. The dog is cared for at the checkpoint until it is flown back to the musher's handlers.

Gangline — A line (cable) that runs the length of the dogs to the front leaders. It connects the team of dogs to the sled. All dogs are attached on either side of the gangline by tug lines. This is the main connection that allows the dogs to pull the sled safely.

Gee — The command for a right turn.

Haw — The command for a left turn.

Jumble ice — Sometimes a river freezes, melts, and then refreezes. The water flowing underneath the ice can exert pressure. This can force pieces to separate and then refreeze irregularly, in a jumble.

Lead dogs or Leaders — Especially intelligent and fast dogs who run in first position.

Neck line — The line that connects a dog's collar to the gangline and between the two collars of a double lead.

Snow hook — A heavy piece of metal with U-shaped prongs and sharp points like teeth that are attached to the sled by a cable. The snow hook is embedded in the snow and then stomped on. This can hold the team and the sled for a short period of time.

Snub line — A rope attached to the sled that is used to tie the sled to a tree or other object.

Tug line — A line that connects a dog's harness to the gangline.

Wheel dogs or Wheelers — The dogs placed directly in front of the sled. Their job is to pull the sled out and around corners or trees.

Thank you to the educational website, Iditarod EDU (https://iditarod.com/edu/what-those-mushing-words-mean/), which provided many of these definitions.

Thinking about
ALASKA! Danger on the Mushing Trail

1. Brent fed honey balls to his dogs as a treat. What would you mix into a treat for your sled dogs?

2. What happened to Atasak's father? Why was she worried?

3. How did Josh feel when Brent wanted him to put medicine on Popsicle's paw? How would you have felt?

4. Why do you think Josh finally said yes to a lesson in mushing?

5. How did Hank show how competitive he was?

6. When Hank was injured on the trail, what did he blame his accident on? Why?

7. Why did Brent and Josh have trouble believing that story?

8. Why was Josh worried about Hank's wound?

9. How was Josh able to move Hank to the sled?

10. What was the low hum and then a growling, clattering noise that Josh heard as he was trying to get Hank home? Why was that dangerous?

11. How did Brent feel after the county finals race at the end of the book? Why?

12. Where would you like Josh and Lizzie to go next?

For additional parent/teacher discussion questions, please visit: https://barbaralarmonfailing.com

Acknowledgments

A very special thank you to the following people:

My husband, Robert, and my son, Gates, for listening patiently and discussing character and plot ideas.

Louise Failing, Susan Hobson, Colbie Michael Magliano, Susan Masters, and Michele Noiset for their patience in reading and rereading multiple versions of this story and taking the time to discuss (seemingly) endless details.

Friends (old and new) and family (you know who you are!) who have been enormously supportive throughout this process.

Angie Taggert, my friend from Ketchikan, Alaska, who ran the Iditarod in 2011 and read through the manuscript for authenticity. Her input was essential and very much appreciated.

Erik Drohman, illustrator/graphic designer, for his superb cover, illustrations, book design, and fantastic collaboration.

Pam Glauber for her skilled developmental editing, insight into the characters, and the arc of this story.

Jane Holmes, director of education at https://iditarod.com

About the Author

Barbara Larmon Failing is the author of *Lasso Lou and Cowboy McCoy*, *Summer Success,* and *School Success*. For over twenty years, she taught first and fifth grades, and she has reviewed children's books for Parent ABCs and The Press of Atlantic City.

Part of a US Public Health Service family, Barbara has lived in many areas of the United States, including New England, the Mid-Atlantic region, the Midwest, the West Coast, and Alaska. She now lives in the Midwest with her family. Writing and traveling are two of her passions.

A portion of the proceeds from the Adventure USA series will be donated to support the work of

"Every family deserves to thrive and be hopeful about their future. That's why One Dublin empowers the community to help one another in times of need to make sure our kids have what they need and to keep a small crisis from becoming a big one."
Heather Heins, Executive Director

"The *Jean Griffith Back-to-School Celebration* provides free backpacks and school supplies for students in need. The goal is to not only provide basic school supplies, but to allow students to pick out their own backpack so they are ready and excited for their first day of school."

To learn more about One Dublin, including ways to volunteer or help, please visit their website: https://one-dublin.org/

Interested in the next book in the Adventure USA series? Here's the first chapter of

By Barbara Larmon Failing
Scheduled to be published in **Fall/Winter 2023**

Chapter 1
M/V Eagle Ferry to Nantucket

Eleven-year-old twins, Josh and Lizzie Parker, dashed up the staircase of the *M/V Eagle*.

"We're almost to Nantucket," said Lizzie.

Josh nodded. "I can't wait to dock."

Stepping onto the upper deck, the twins almost collided with a red-haired man dressed in khakis and a starched shirt who had a phone pressed against his ear. His trousers were tucked into a pair of leather sailing boots. He stood out from the rest of the passengers who were dressed casually in shorts, T-shirts, and sandals.

A deep frown plastered to his face, he snarled to the twins, "Watch where you're going!" before returning to his phone.

ADVENTURE USA

"I need payment now!" he hissed into the phone. "The loan is overdue!"

"That's one angry tourist," Josh whispered.

"People are supposed to be happy on vacation," Lizzie added.

"We are!" said Josh.

The twins paused to read a chart describing the features of the *M/V Eagle*.

"She's 230 feet long and carries 1,000 passengers," said Lizzie.

"Plus, fifty-three cars, seven semis, and four regular trucks," said Josh.

At the railing, the twins found a bench with two open seats. The wind ruffled their hair as they breathed the salty air. Lizzie pulled her long, wavy brown hair into a ponytail to keep it from blowing in her face. Their parents had driven to the ferry terminal in Hyannis, a town midway to the "elbow" of Cape Cod. After two hours aboard the *Eagle*, they were almost to the Steamship Authority Terminal in downtown Nantucket.

Lizzie took out her phone. "I want to film that lighthouse you talked about."

"Brant Point," said Josh. "We should be able to spot it soon."

Overhead, gulls circled. A few swooped down to the deck hoping to get a piece of food. One almost carried off Lizzie's bag of popcorn, but she snatched it back just in time.

"They're not getting my lunch!" Josh quickly stashed his sandwich back in the cooler.

"I wish people wouldn't feed them," Lizzie said. "It only encourages them to try harder."

Josh peered through his binoculars. "There's the lighthouse!"

"Let me see!" cried Lizzie.

"It's the second oldest lighthouse in the US," he explained. "Built in 1746. It used to have a Fresnel lens before it was automated."

"A fuzzy what?"

"Fresnel," Josh repeated. "Augustin Fresnel invented it. The lens is like a beehive with a bunch of glass prisms bending the light and magnifying it. It's super efficient. The bright light can be seen many miles away."

"You and your facts," said Lizzie. "Knock, knock."

"Who's there?"

"Orange."

"Orange who?" said Josh.

"Orange you glad Mom and Dad chose to research Nantucket for their blog?"

"Absolutely. This is awesome!"

"Listen for the foghorn booming as soon as we pass Brant Point." Josh pressed his Phillies ball cap firmly over his blond curly hair and rested the binoculars on his chest. "It's got a very

ADVENTURE USA

low pitch which means a long wavelength. The sound travels several miles."

He'd barely stopped speaking when the deep, mournful sound of the foghorn rumbled across the water.

Lizzie moved to the railing. The ferry was approaching the lighthouse. She took out her phone to film it.

"You sure have your facts down," an older woman near them said. "Are you visitors or natives?"

"First time on the island," said Josh. "We're super excited."

"You're lucky you didn't come yesterday," the woman said. "High winds from the hurricane down south caused a lot of ferry cancellations. The wind whipped up the waves."

"We like wild weather," said Lizzie, returning to her seat.

"Then watch out for rip currents," the woman said.

"I've heard of them," said Josh. "They're a strong, narrow current in a specific area near beaches, right?"

"Exactly," she went on. "The current moves away from the beach like a swift river heading out to sea. It's strongest on the surface."

The woman smoothed her white hair away from her face. "Welcome to Nantucket! I'm Sara Coleman Clarke. But everyone calls me Grams." Her eyes twinkled. "I'm sort of a grandmother to the island children."

"Cool," said Lizzie. "I'm Lizzie Parker. And this is my twin brother, Josh."

M/V Eagle Ferry to Nantucket

"We've been reading about whaling in Nantucket," said Josh.

"Our parents have a travel blog," Lizzie said. "We're here to explore while they work."

"You're about the age of my granddaughter," Grams said. "She would be happy to show you around."

"Awesome," said Lizzie. She and Josh had been hoping to find friends on the island.

"I've got some fun facts for you," said Grams. "Thomas Mayhew bought the island in the mid-1600s from an English earl. He paid forty pounds and two beaver hats."

Lizzie couldn't help giggling. "What a deal!"

"It sure was. Nantucket means 'far away land' in the Wampanoag language. It's about twenty-nine miles from Hyannis. The Coffins and other Nantucket families started whaling in the late 1600s," Grams went on. "They also ended up discovering many faraway islands."

"Those whaling ships seem super cool," Josh said. "Also, those roof walks at the top of houses."

"You'll want to visit the Coleman Clarke House, my family's museum," Grams continued. "It will help you understand Nantucket."

"It's first on our list," said Josh.

"Plus, you're just in time for the Spyglass Spectacle!" Grams leaned forward as though passing on a secret. "We'll have Reuben Coffin's spyglass on display. First time ever!"

147

"Wow!" said Lizzie.

"It's priceless," explained Grams. "We've had to substantially increase our insurance in case—heaven forbid—something should happen to it. But it's worth it. We're hoping for a big turnout. The museum needs a lot of updating to stay open. And increasing our endowment would keep us open for years to come."

Grams lifted her purse to her lap, rummaged through it, and pulled out a brochure. "Here's some information about things to do." She tucked two pieces of paper inside. "And two free tickets to the museum to get you started on your adventures. Ask for me when you arrive, and I can introduce you to Zoey."

The twins' eyes lit up. "Thanks so much!"

Grams winked at the twins as she stood. "See you soon, I hope."

www.ingramcontent.com/pod-product-compliance
Lightning Source LLC
Chambersburg PA
CBHW022036220526
45357CB00059B/284